LAST OF THE SANDWALKERS

WRITTEN AND ILLUSTRATED BY
JAY HOSLER

:01

First Second
New York

First Second

Copyright © 2015 by Jay Hosler
Published by First Second
First Second is an imprint of Roaring Brook Press, a division of Holtzbrinck
Publishing Holdings Limited Partnership
175 Fifth Avenue, New York, New York 10010

Cataloging-in-Publication Data is on file at the Library of Congress

ISBN: 978-1-62672-024-4

First Second books may be purchased for business or promotional use. For
information on bulk purchases please contact Macmillan Corporate and Premium
Sales Department at (800) 221-7945 x5442 or by email at specialmarkets@
macmillan.com.

FIRST
EDITION

First edition 2015

Book design by Colleen AF Venable and Andrew Arnold
Printed in the United States of America by RR Donnelley & Sons Company,
Crawfordsville, Indiana

10 9 8 7 6 5 4 3 2 1

BY ART
WE LIVE

This book is a loving tribute to my mom and dad, Madonna and Scott Hosler, and the family they made.

Many, many people helped to make this book better over the ten plus years I have been working on it. I owe my deepest gratitude to Lisa, Max, and Jack Hosler for reading everything multiple times and giving me their unvarnished opinions. I am also thankful for the discerning eyes of Dave, Rebecca, and Benjamin Hsiung, Laura and Jamie White, Belle and Jim Tuten, Cathy Stenson, Matt Powell, Jim Ottaviani, John Kerschbaum, Zander Cannon, Craig Fisher, Joe Sutliff Sanders, Jarod Rosello, Daryn Guarino, and Troy Cummings. Finally, I deeply appreciate the guidance, support, patience, and all-around kindness of Calista Brill, Colleen Venable, and Gina Gagliano at First Second.

A GUIDE TO IDENTIFYING BEETLES

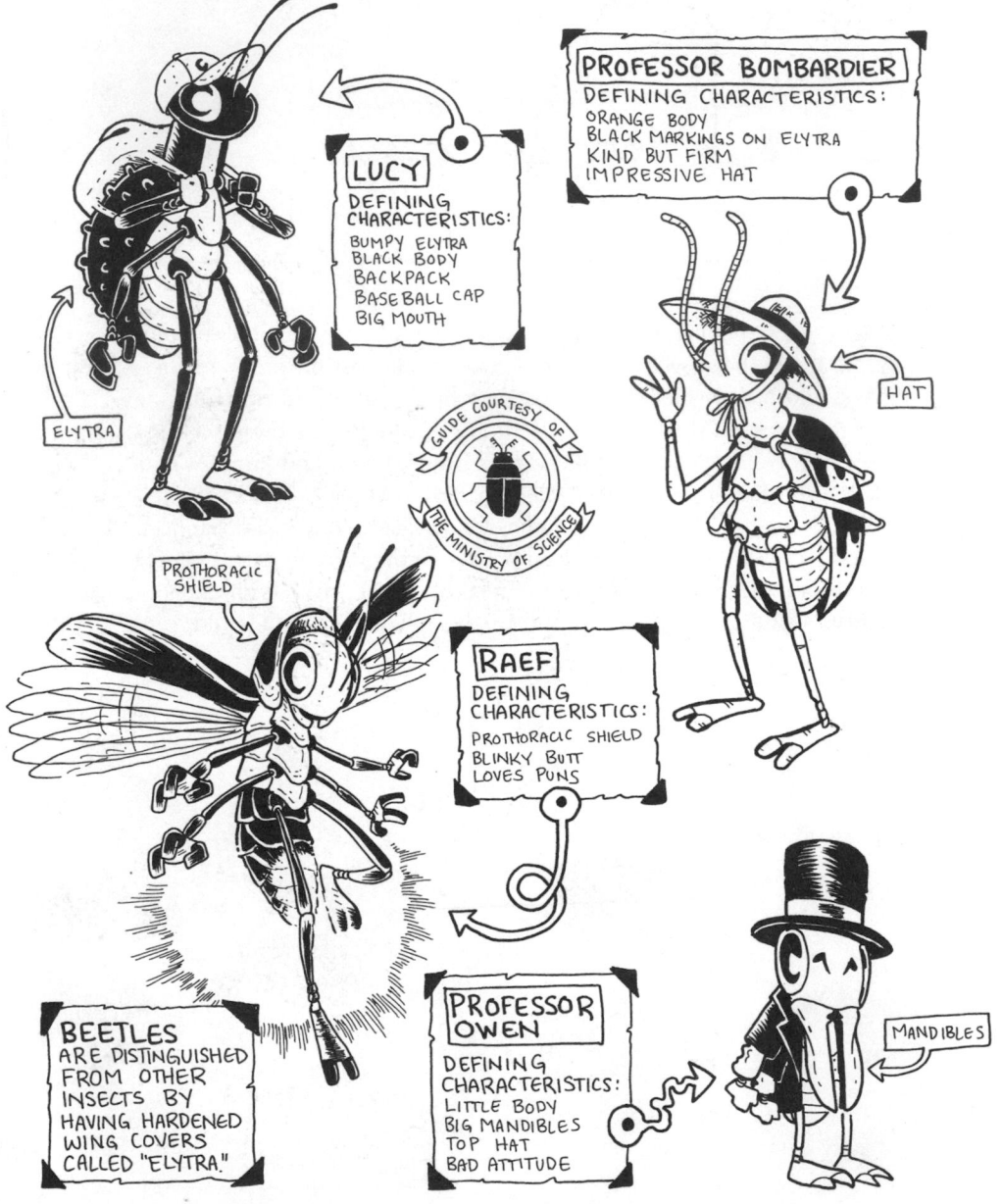

LUCY
DEFINING CHARACTERISTICS:
BUMPY ELYTRA
BLACK BODY
BACKPACK
BASEBALL CAP
BIG MOUTH

PROFESSOR BOMBARDIER
DEFINING CHARACTERISTICS:
ORANGE BODY
BLACK MARKINGS ON ELYTRA
KIND BUT FIRM
IMPRESSIVE HAT

ELYTRA

HAT

GUIDE COURTESY OF
THE MINISTRY OF SCIENCE

PROTHORACIC SHIELD

RAEF
DEFINING CHARACTERISTICS:
PROTHORACIC SHIELD
BLINKY BUTT
LOVES PUNS

BEETLES
ARE DISTINGUISHED FROM OTHER INSECTS BY HAVING HARDENED WING COVERS CALLED "ELYTRA."

PROFESSOR OWEN
DEFINING CHARACTERISTICS:
LITTLE BODY
BIG MANDIBLES
TOP HAT
BAD ATTITUDE

MANDIBLES

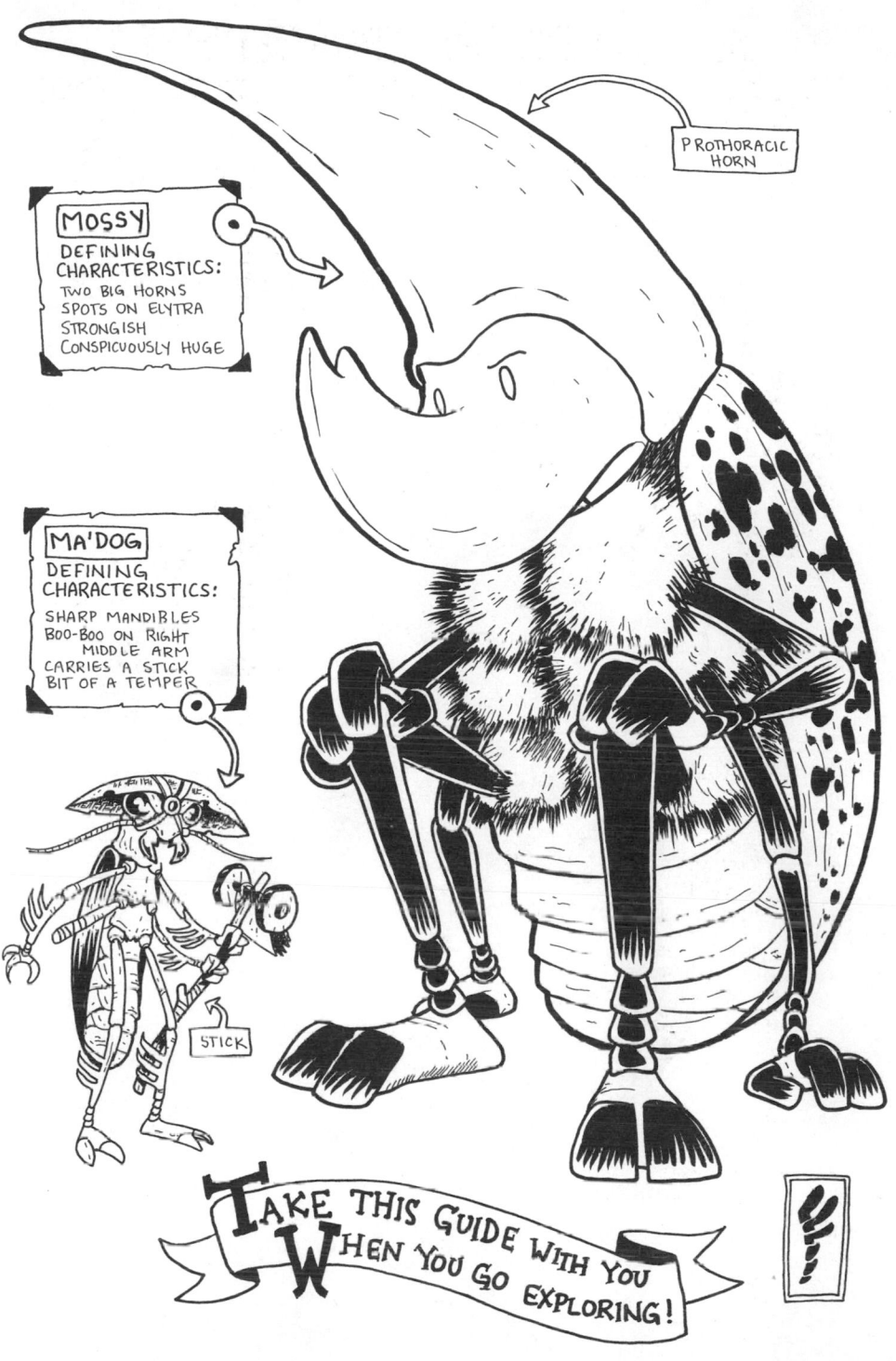

Chapter 1

LEADING THE FIRST MISSION TO SEEK OUT LIFE BEYOND OUR OASIS SHOULD HAVE BEEN THE GREATEST MOMENT OF MY SCIENTIFIC CAREER. INSTEAD, WE SHUFFLED OUT OF TOWN LIKE WRAITHS THROUGH THE MORNING MISTS. IT'S JUST AS WELL, THOUGH, SINCE MOST OF OUR COLLEAGUES ARE CONVINCED WE WILL FAIL.

WE PASSED THROUGH THE GREAT WESTERN GATE IN SILENCE.

BY MIDDAY WE PASSED WITHIN VIEW OF THE RUINS OF OLD COLEOPOLIS. OUR MELANCHOLY MOOD WAS IMMEDIATELY BURNED AWAY BY THE SIGHT. AS FAR AS I KNOW, WE WERE THE FIRST BEETLES IN A MILLENIUM TO SET EYES ON THEM.

THE CITY WAS DESTROYED OVER A THOUSAND YEARS AGO BY THREE COCONUTS THAT FELL FROM A SHELTERING PALM TREE.

LEGEND HAS IT THAT THE GOD SCARABUS CAST DOWN THE COCONUTS TO PUNISH THE INHABITANTS FOR WHAT HE CONSIDERED AN UNHEALTHY QUEST FOR KNOWLEDGE.

EVERYTHING WAS DEMOLISHED, INCLUDING THE LEGENDARY LIBRARY. THE HANDFUL OF BEETLES THAT SURVIVED WISELY CHOSE TO ESTABLISH NEW COLEOPOLIS FAR AWAY FROM ANY TREES.

IT'S AN AMAZING THING TO BEHOLD.

OF COURSE, I WAS STRUCK BY THE FACT THAT WE COULD SEE THE RUINS AT **ALL**. HOW IS IT THAT AFTER A THOUSAND YEARS THE OLD CITY ISN'T **COMPLETELY** OVERGROWN?

I'D LOVE TO INVESTIGATE, BUT GOING THERE IS FORBIDDEN. OUR RULERS DON'T WANT TO RISK PROVOKING SCARABUS AGAIN.

A DISTANT GLIMPSE IS ALL WE GET.

A FEW HOURS LATER, WE WERE AT THE EDGE OF THE OASIS AND FACING A HORIZON FULL OF SAND.

OUR MISSION IS TO LOOK FOR LIFE IN THIS VAST NOTHINGNESS. THIS WAS MY IDEA. MY PLAN. AND AT THAT MOMENT, IT SEEMED **INSANE**.

IMPOSSIBLE.

STUPID.

TERRIFYING.

BUT THEN I TOOK MY FIRST STEP INTO THE DESERT SAND AND I HAD THE STRANGEST FEELING THAT I WAS...

...HOME.

WITH THAT, MY DOUBTS EVAPORATED. I WALKED INTO THE DESERT AND **NEVER LOOKED BACK**.

(OKAY, I LOOKED BACK **ONCE**, BUT THAT WAS JUST TO TELL RAEF TO HURRY UP.)

LUCY'S JOURNAL
FEB. 17, 1002

I DON'T KNOW WHAT I WAS EXPECTING, BUT IT WASN'T **THIS**. WE'VE SEEN NOTHING BUT SAND.

WE'VE STOPPED FOR THE DAY, AND MOSSY HAS PLANTED OUR BANNER AT THE EDGE OF CAMP.

(IT BEARS THE ANTENNA ICON, OUR SYMBOL OF SCIENTIFIC DISCOVERY.)

IT'S A HOPEFUL ACT THAT HELPS ME DEAL WITH THE DESPAIR I'M STARTING TO FEEL.

IT'S TWILIGHT NOW, AND, AS USUAL, AN ANXIOUS STILLNESS PERMEATES THE GROUP. EVEN THOUGH WE'VE SURVIVED TWO NIGHTS OF CHILL-COMA, WE'RE ALL STILL A BIT NERVOUS WHEN THE SUN GOES DOWN.

THE FRIGID DESERT NIGHT WILL LEAVE US IMMOBILIZED AND HELPLESS.

I THINK I WAS PREPARED FOR THE GRUELING PHYSICAL CHALLENGES OF THIS TRIP, BUT I DIDN'T ANTICIPATE THE EMOTIONAL TOLL IT WOULD EXACT. LIKE THE DESERT TEMPERATURES, I SWING FROM HOT TO COLD. I SPEND THE DAY EXCITED, HUNGRY TO FIND SOMETHING NEW.

AND I SPEND EACH NIGHT TERRIFIED...

Chapter 2

GOOD MORNING, TEAM. CAN ANYONE MOVE YET?
NOPE.
NOT YET, DEAR.
HOW 'BOUT YOU, RAEF?
RAEF?
RAEF, DEAR, ARE YOU AWAKE?
RAEF?
RAEF!
OKAY, LET'S NOT PANIC.
CAN YOU GET TO HIM, LUCY?
I'LL... TRY...

CONGRATULATIONS, LUCY, YOUR SOLAR CHARGED DESERT COCOONS HAVE WORKED THREE NIGHTS IN A ROW.

YEP. WE HAVEN'T FROZEN TO DEATH ONCE!

AND, BASED ON THE FACT THAT WE WEREN'T EATEN, PROF. BOMBARDIER'S CHEMICAL TREATMENT OF THE COCOONS SEEMS TO HAVE DETERRED ANY NOCTURNAL DESERT MONSTERS.

SHEESH. WHAT A WAY TO START THE DAY: NOXIOUS AND IMMOBILE.

YOU'LL GET USED TO IT, RAEF.

I'LL NEVER GET USED TO SLIPPING INTO A COMA WHENEVER I GET TOO COLD.

I THINK IT'S KINDA PEACEFUL.

ARE YOU KIDDING ME?

IT'S TOTALLY FREAKY!

oh, no...

LOOKS LIKE RAEF CAN MOVE.

oh, c'mon, guys, please, not again.

13

YOU KNOW THE RULE: FIRST ONE TO MOVE HAS TO CHECK ON PROFESSOR OWEN.

BUT LUCY MOVED FIRST!

ONLY BECAUSE YOU TRICKED HER.

I THOUGHT YOU WERE **DEAD!**

WELL, NOW I WISH I **WERE.**

I'M STARTING TO WORRY RAEF'S MEMORY IS NEVER GONNA RETURN.

GIVE HIM TIME, LUCY.

IT'S STILL EARLY.

sigh.

PROFESSOR OWEN?

IS THE TEA READY?

NO, SIR.

LUCY HASN'T COLLECTED THE WATER, YET.

THEN WHY ARE YOU BOTHERING ME?

GET OUT.

GO!

ZIP

SLOW DOWN, RAEF, THERE'S NO ONE BEHIND YOU.

GEE WHIZ, THAT GUY **HATES** ME!

OH, POOH.

HE TREATS EVERYONE THAT WAY.

YEAH, BUT HE DOES HAVE A SPECIAL SOUR SPOT FOR US.

WHY?

IT'S A LONG STORY, DEAR.

SHOOT, I'M STILL SURPRISED HE APPROVED FUNDING FOR THIS EXPEDITION.

AND WHY DID HE WANT TO COME WITH US? HE'S BEEN NOTHING BUT A PAIN IN THE ABDOMEN.

YEAH, HE'S A CREEP, BUT HE'S THE CREEP IN CHARGE OF THE SCIENCE MINISTRY, SO, IF HE WANTS TO COME, HE CAN COME.

ANYWAY, FORGET THAT OLD GROUCH, LET'S CHECK THE WATER TRAPS.

I'VE GOT THE CANTEENS.

THE FOG IS THICK THIS MORNING. I HOPE WE COLLECTED A BUNCH.

LOOKS LIKE ANOTHER SUCCESSFUL INVENTION, LUCY.

THEY'RE COMPLETELY FULL.

I THINK I'LL CELEBRATE BY GETTING MY MORNING WATER THE OLD-FASHIONED WAY.

OOH! THIS IS SUCH A FASCINATING PROCESS!

YEAH, DOC, YOU TELL US ABOUT IT EVERY MORNING.

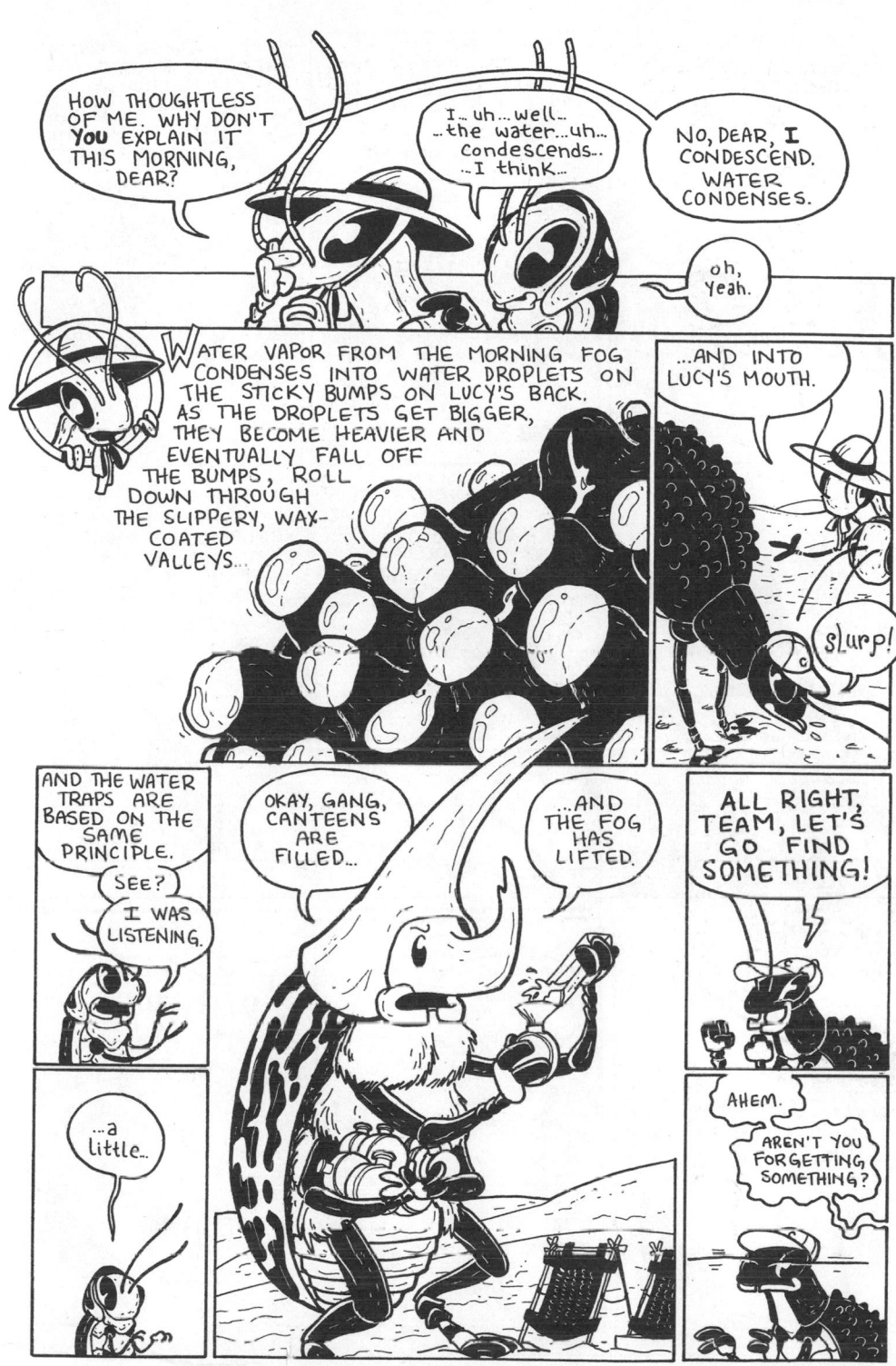

GOOD MORNING, PROFESSOR OWEN. I WAS JUST COMING TO...

THE CEREMONIAL TRACHEAL HORNS HAVE NOT BEEN BLOWN TO ANNOUNCE THE DAY.

Riiight.

SEE, I FIGURED SINCE IT GETS HOT SO QUICKLY THAT IT WOULD BE A BETTER USE OF OUR TIME TO **SKIP** THE HORNS THIS MORNING.

YOU FIGURED?

WELL, LET'S HOPE THAT THIS IS NOT THE FIRST IN A LONG STRING OF MISCALCULATIONS. AS THE QUEEN'S REPRESENTATIVE ON THIS EXPEDITION, I MUST **INSIST** ON FOLLOWING CEREMONIAL PROTOCOL. AS TEAM LEADER, THAT RESPONSIBILITY FALLS TO YOU.

I...

THE TEMPERATURE IS RISING, "PROFESSOR." I SUGGEST YOU GET STARTED.

...mumble mumble...

RAEF! WHERE IS MY TEA?

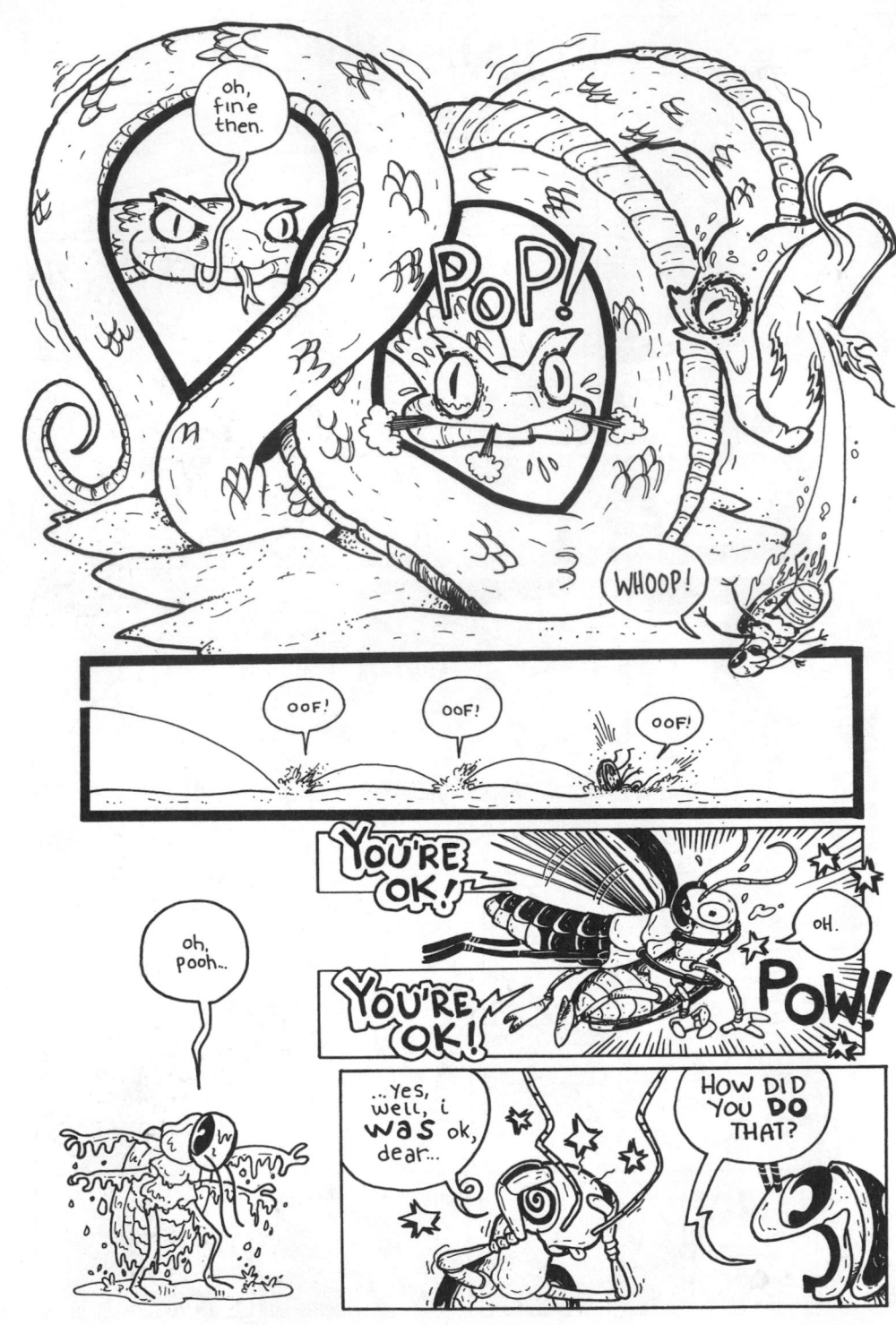

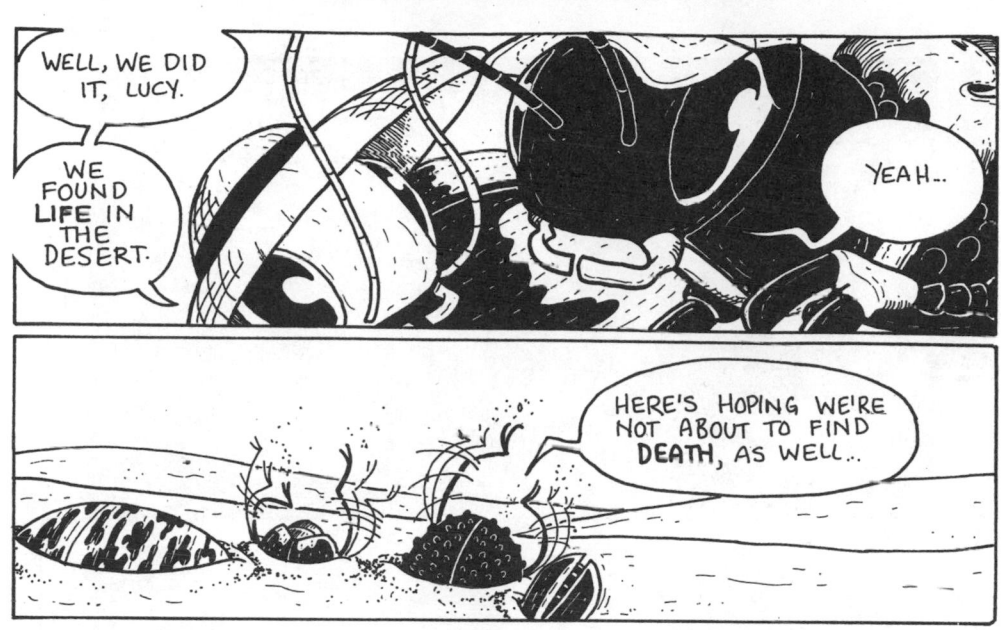

WELL, WE DID IT, LUCY.

WE FOUND **LIFE** IN THE DESERT.

YEAH..

HERE'S HOPING WE'RE NOT ABOUT TO FIND **DEATH**, AS WELL..

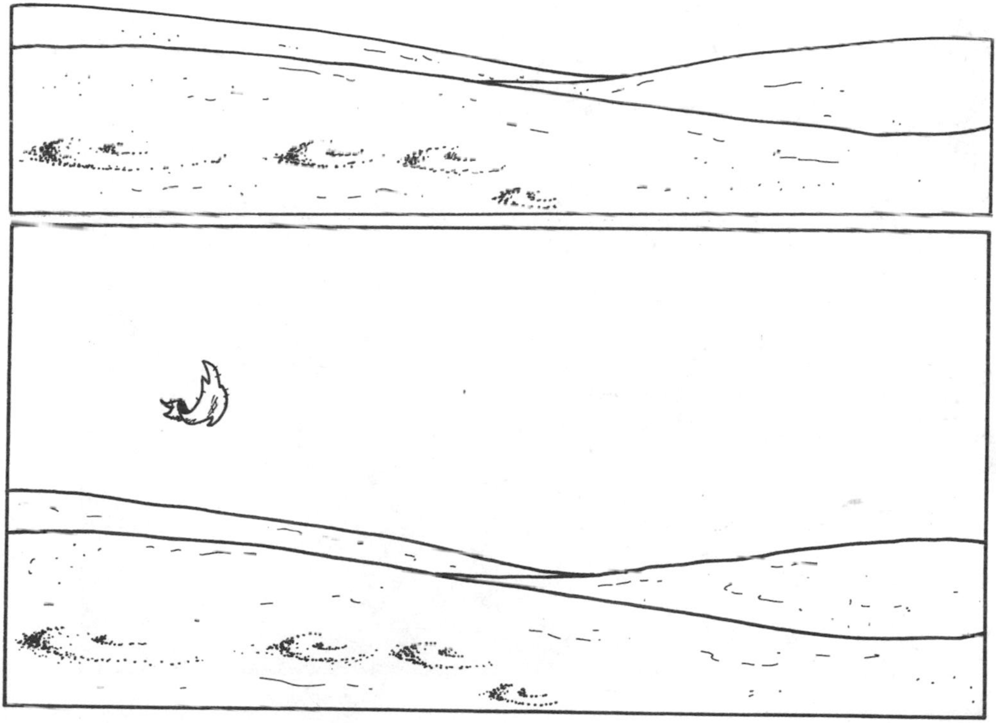

Chapter 3

FAN OUT AND COLLECT WHAT SUPPLIES YOU CAN FIND.

it's over.

DO YOU REALIZE WHAT YOU'VE DONE?

SAVED YOUR LIFE,"SIR"?

YOU HAVE FORFEITED YOUR LIFE'S DREAM. LOSING THE SUPPLIES WAS BAD ENOUGH, BUT ALLOWING THAT BEHEMOTH TO **TOUCH** ME...

I HAD TO ACT QUICKLY, PROFESSOR OWEN. OR YOU—

DO NOT INSULT MY INTELLIGENCE!

HUMILIATING ME COMES AT A HIGH PRICE.

I'M CANCELLING THE EXPEDITION.

YOU CAN'T DO THAT!

THE QUEEN HERSELF...

APPROVED THIS ENDEAVOR DESPITE MY OBJECTIONS. **BUT** SHE GAVE ME FULL AUTHORITY AND WHEN SHE HEARS OF YOUR DISRESPECTFUL BEHAVIOR...

but...

YOU AREN'T **ENTIRELY** TO BLAME, OF COURSE. SOMEONE WITH YOUR LOW BREEDING COULD **HARDLY** BE EXPECTED TO BE ANYTHING BUT ILL MANNERED.

HMM. I WONDER IF THE COMPLETE FAILURE OF THIS VERY EXPENSIVE EXPEDITION WILL COST YOU YOUR FACULTY POSITION, LUCY?

tsk. Oh, well...

I EXPECT YOU TO SIGNAL THE RETRIEVAL TEAMS WITHIN THE HOUR.

RRRRRRRRRRRRRRRRR

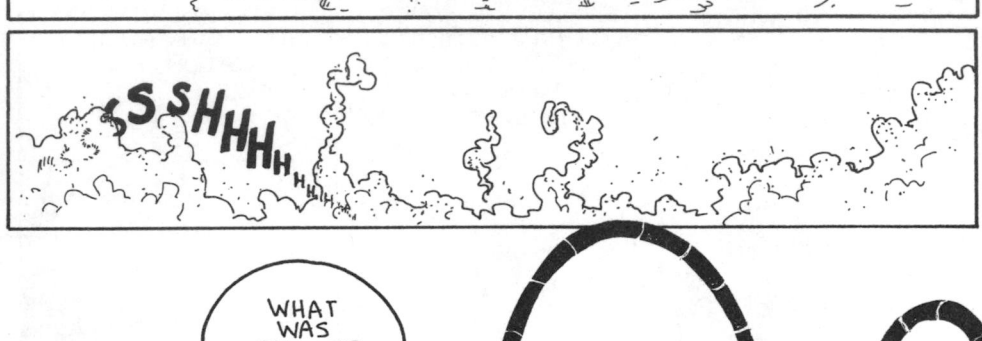

LUCY?

DO YOU SEE ANYTHING, RAEF?

NOT YET.

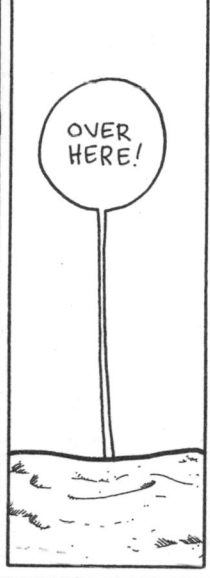

OVER HERE!

HI, GUYS!

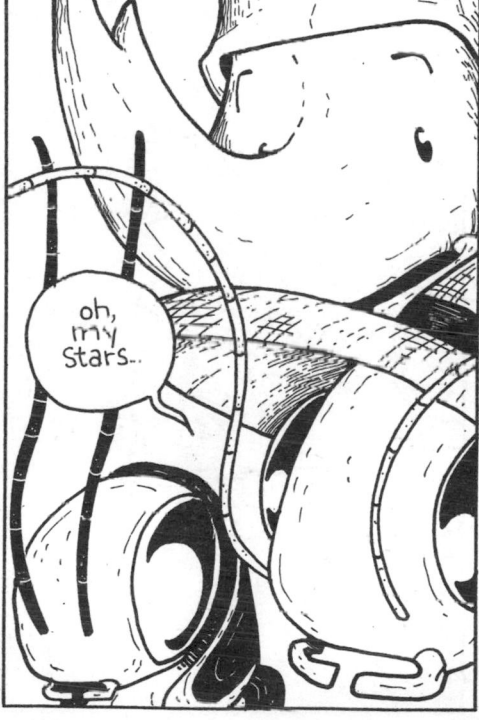

oh, my stars...

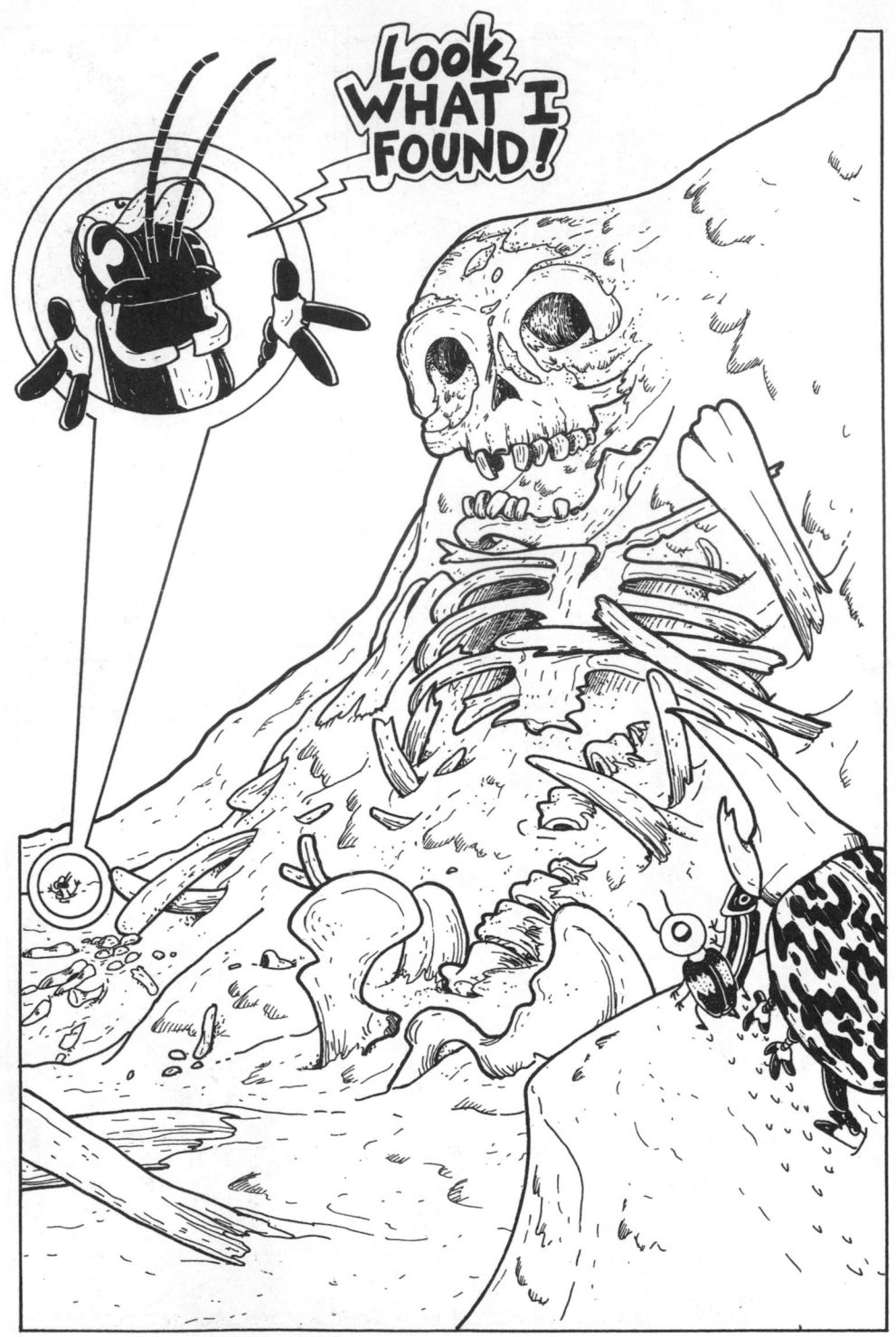

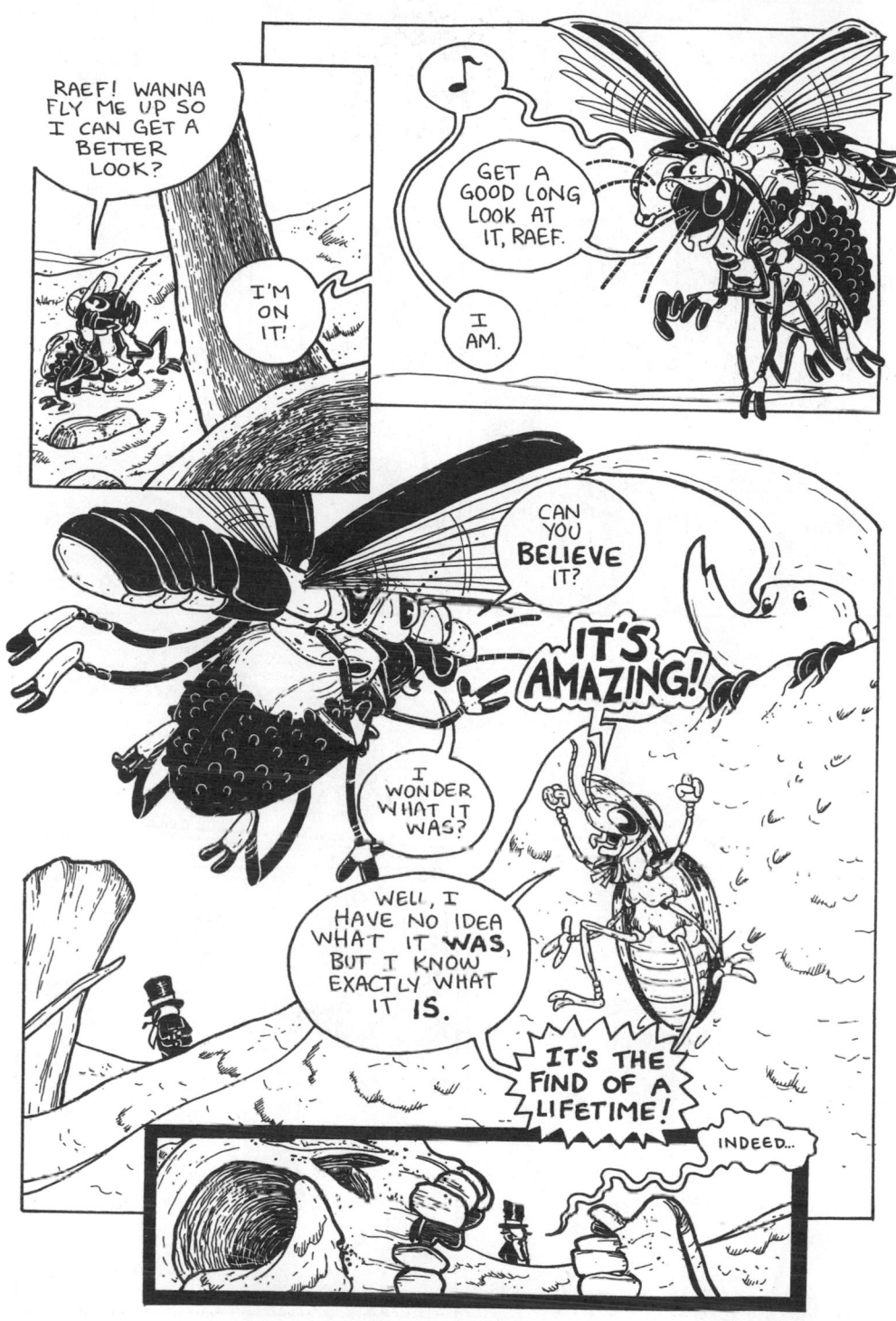

OKAY, GANG, LET'S RELEASE THESE PHEROMONE FLARES AND GET CRACKIN'. THE RETRIEVAL MOTHS COULD BE HERE AS EARLY AS TOMORROW MORNING SO WE NEED TO MAKE A COMPLETE RECORD OF EVERYTHING VISIBLE BEFORE NIGHT FALL.

Y'KNOW, LUCE, THIS IS MY LEAST FAVORITE OF YOUR INVENTIONS. THOSE MALE MOTHS ARE GOING TO HOME IN ON THIS FEMALE SCENT LOOKING FOR LOVE... AND WHAT ARE THEY GONNA FIND?

HARD WORK.

WELL, WHAT SHOULD THEY EXPECT?

LOVE IS HARD WORK.

HEY, PROFESSOR, I JUST REALIZED: "LOVE IS IN THE AIR"! HA HA!

KEEP WORKING, DEAR.

WE'RE ALL DONE. YOU COMIN', LUCKY LOO?

WHIP!

WHA-? uh... YEAH, RAEF. ...be right there...

I DON'T SMELL ANYTHING.

YOU'RE NOT A MOTH.

DID YOU HEAR WHAT HE CALLED ME, MOSSY?

YEP. THINGS ARE LOOKIN' UP, LUCY.

42

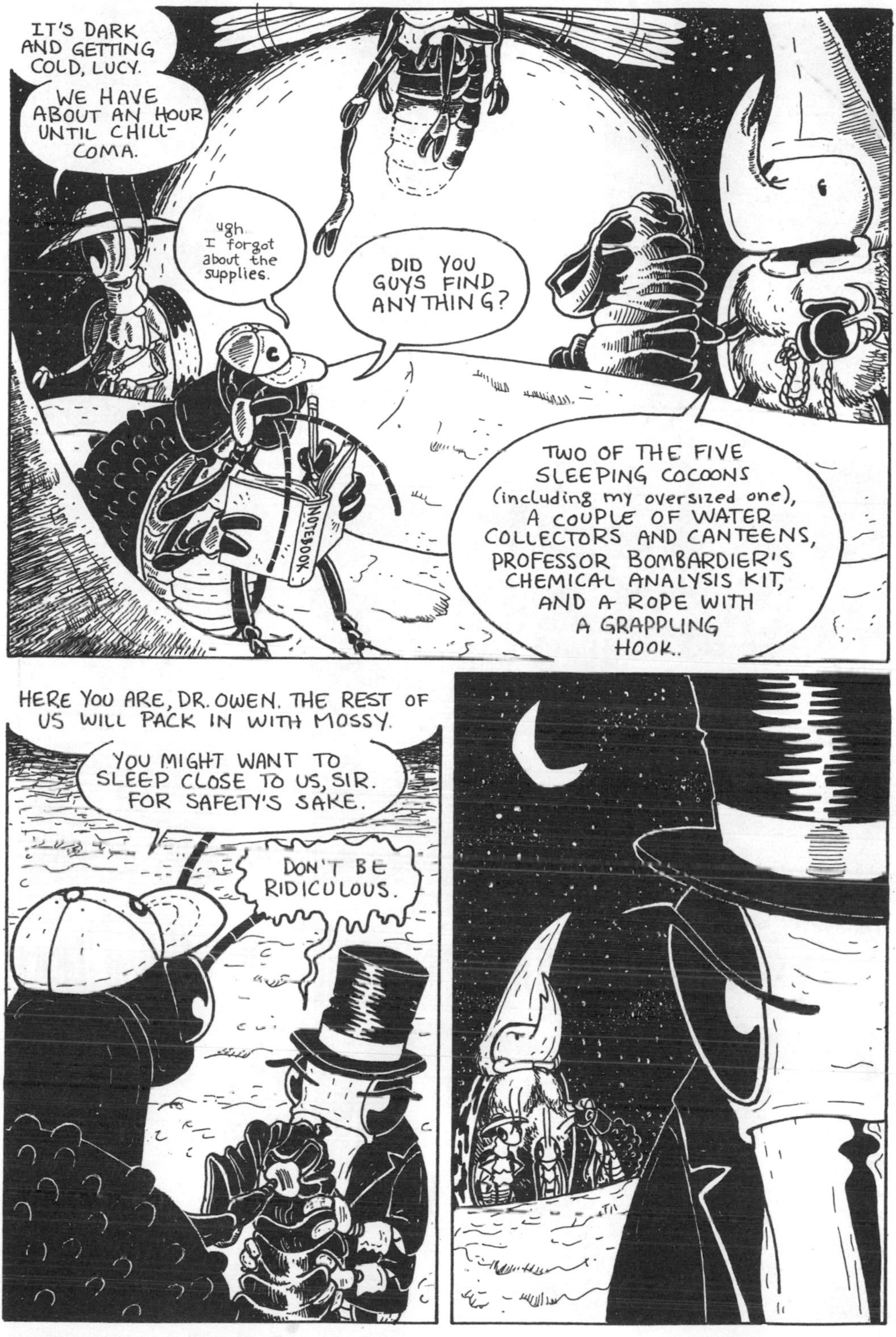

It's dark and getting cold, Lucy.

We have about an hour until chill-coma.

Ugh. I forgot about the supplies.

Did you guys find anything?

Two of the five sleeping cocoons (including my oversized one), a couple of water collectors and canteens, professor Bombardier's chemical analysis kit, and a rope with a grappling hook.

Here you are, Dr. Owen. The rest of us will pack in with Mossy.

You might want to sleep close to us, sir. For safety's sake.

Don't be ridiculous.

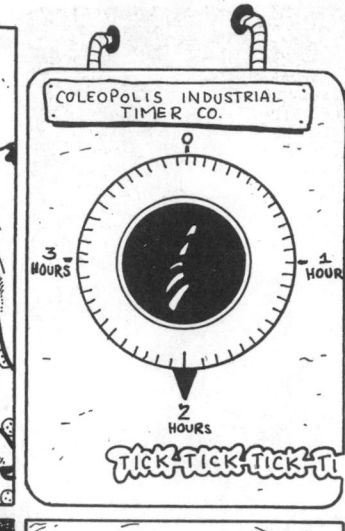

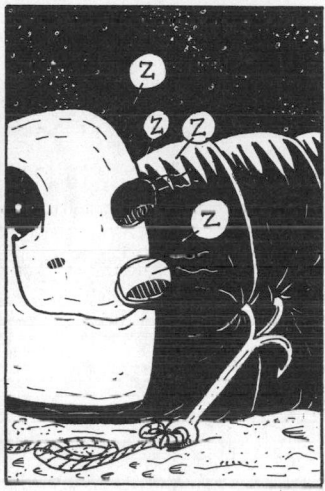

THINK! TRY TO REMEMBER WHO YOU WERE.

THAT THING, WHATEVER IT IS, COULD MAKE US RICH AND FAMOUS.

BUT... THIS IS LUCY'S DISCOVERY.

FORGET ABOUT HER! FORGET ABOUT ALL OF THEM!

I... I COULDN'T DO THAT.

THEY'RE LIKE... FAMILY TO ME.

Sigh. YOU HAVEN'T CHANGED.

YOU'LL NEVER BE THE SAME AGAIN...

WHAT IS THIS ALL ABOUT?

NOTHING. NOTHING.

I JUST NEED YOUR HELP TO MOVE SOMETHING.

FIRST, LET ME TIE THIS AROUND YOUR WAIST.

HOLD ON TO IT VERY TIGHTLY.

UNDERSTAND?

NO.

47

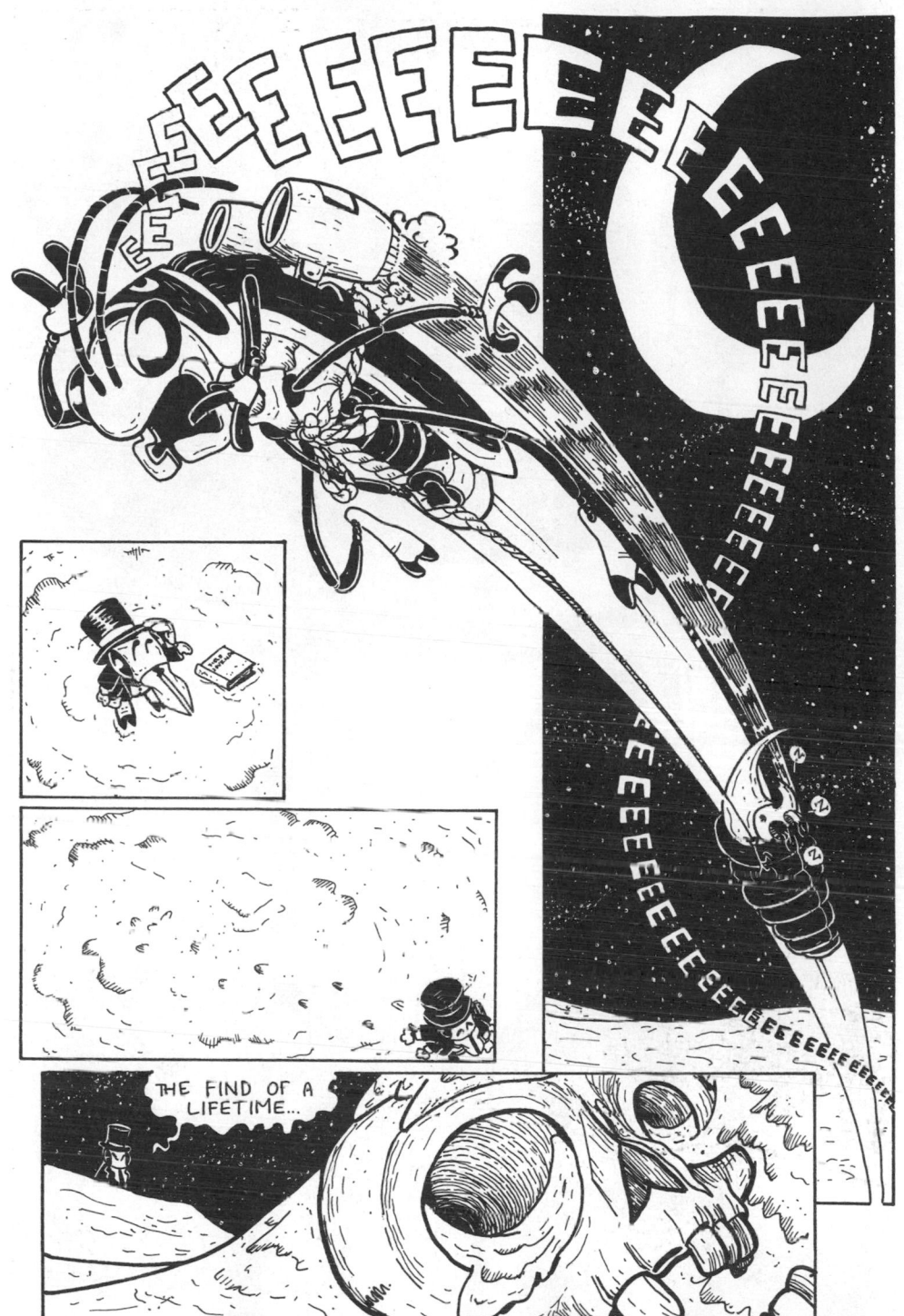

THE FIND OF A LIFETIME...

Chapter 4

WELL, HERE ARE THE FLARES. WHERE'S THE EXPEDITION TEAM?

FAN OUT.

FIND ME SOMETHING.

AND, O'TARSUS?

SIR?

REMEMBER TO ACTIVATE YOUR MOTH'S SLEEP STIMULATOR THIS TIME.

Yes, sir.

"remember to activate your moth's sleep stimulator this time."

ha. ha.

lose one moth and they never let you...

WHAT THE-?

CAPTAIN! HEY, CAPTAIN! CAPTAIN!

CALM DOWN, O'TARSUS. I'M... whoa.

WHAT IS THAT?

IT'S A WARNING FROM SCARABUS, CAPTAIN.

HE IS NOT PLEASED.

WE'RE NOT MONSTERS.

I'M SURE THAT'S WHAT YOU BELIEVE.

UNFORTUNATELY FOR YOU, THAT'S NOT WHAT **I** BELIEVE. SO, NOW THAT THE MORNING DEW HAS DRIED AND IT IS WARM ENOUGH FOR ME TO MOVE, I'M GOING TO EAT YOU.

YOU DON'T WANT TO DO THAT, DEAR.

SORRY, GRANNY, BUT YOU'VE GOT TO BE PROCESSED.

granny?

INSECTS ARE A SWARMING SCOURGE TO LIFE. IT'S A SPIDER'S DUTY TO EXPUNGE YOUR ICKY BADNESS FROM THE WORLD.

WE ARE **NOT** BAD!

BUT WE DO **TASTE** BAD.

THAT'S RIGHT; WE'RE ALSO TOUGH AND CHEWY.

I DON'T PLAN ON CHEWING YOU, SPORT. I'M GONNA LIQUEFY YOUR INSIDES AND SLURP UP YOUR GUTS.

THAT'S A RELIEF. For a minute there i thought we were gonna die horribly...

DON'T FRET, SPARKY. YOU **PROBABLY** WON'T FEEL A THING. THE POISON IN MY BITE WILL PARALYZE YOU, AND THEN I'LL —

TAP

what the..?

YOU... YOU TASTE TERRIBLE!

TOLD YA.

TAP TAP TAP TAP TAP TAP TAP

58

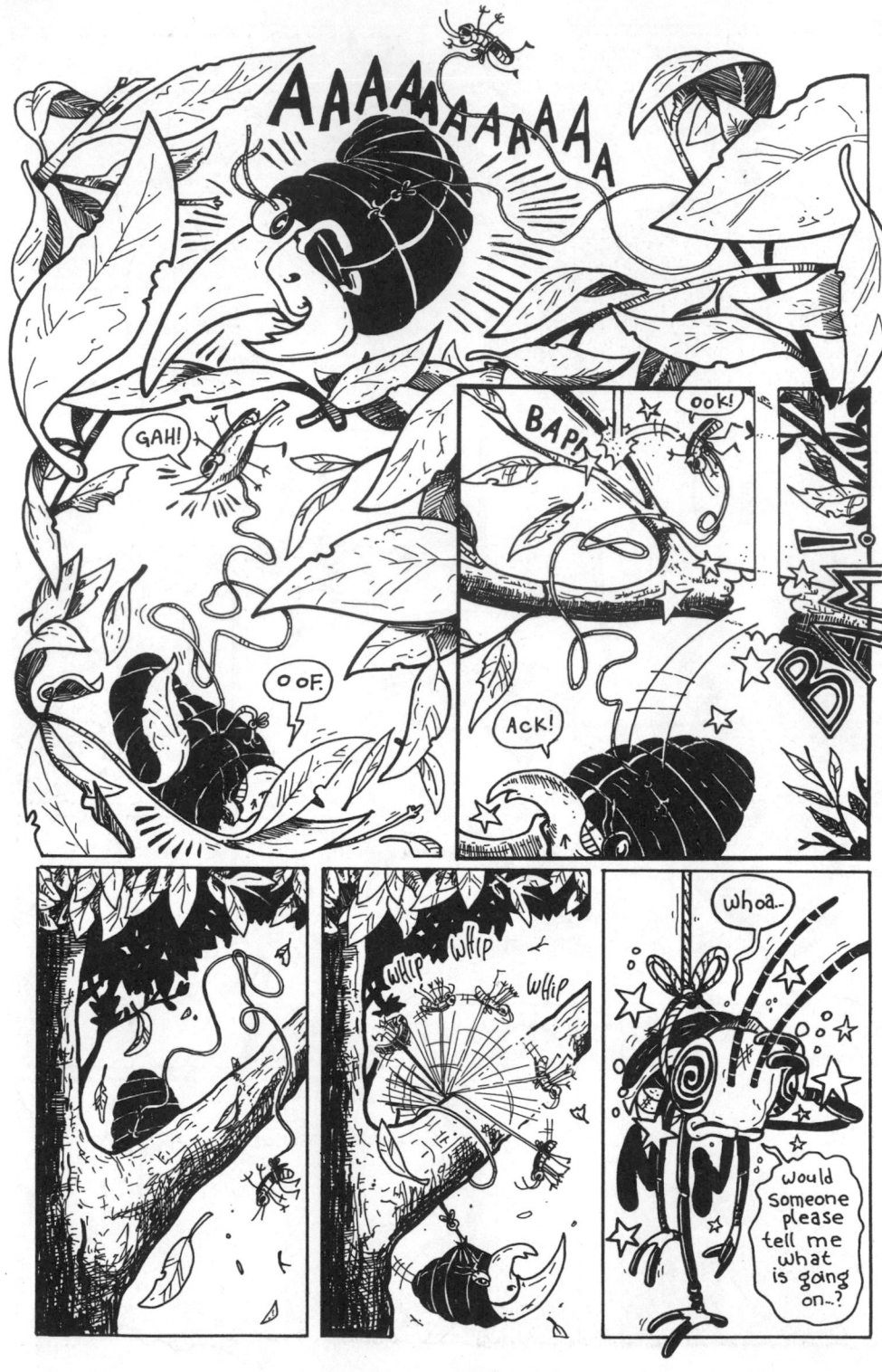

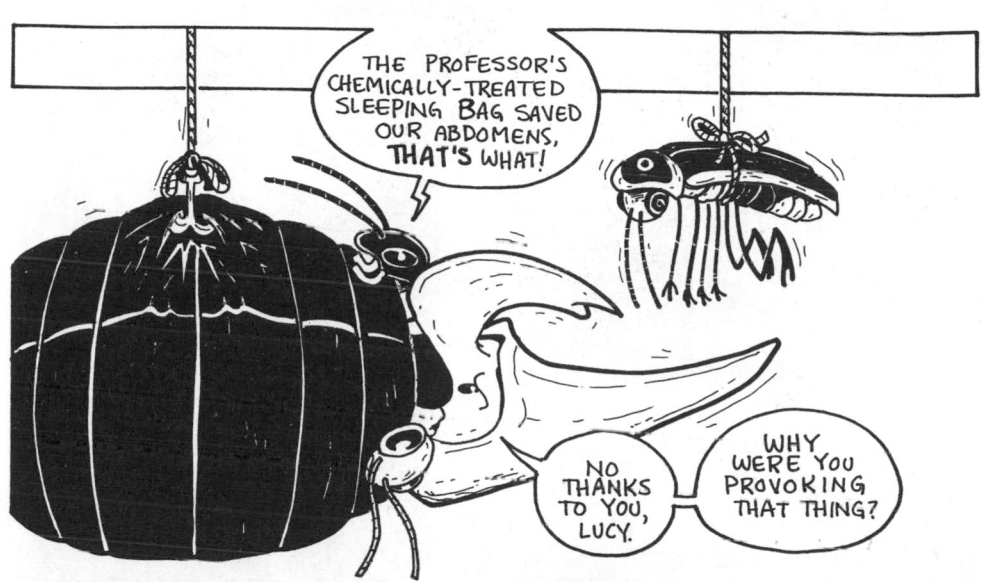

THE PROFESSOR'S CHEMICALLY-TREATED SLEEPING BAG SAVED OUR ABDOMENS, **THAT'S WHAT!**

NO THANKS TO YOU, LUCY.

WHY WERE YOU PROVOKING THAT THING?

IT'S CALLED A DISTRACTION, MOSSY. I DIDN'T WANT IT TO NOTICE THE ROPE AND CUT THAT, TOO!

THE IMPORTANT THING IS THAT WE'RE ALL OKAY.

OKAY?

ROCKETS POP OUT OF MY BACK!

ROCKETS...?

wow, that's—

really?

uh

are you sure?

RIGHT, WELL THEN, I GUESS YOU'RE JUST FULL OF SURPRISES, RAEF.

YOU KNEW, DIDN'T YOU?

DIDN'T YOU?

NOW, LET'S ALL CALM DOWN AND...

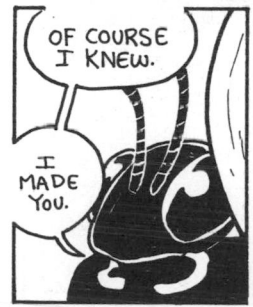

OF COURSE I KNEW.

I MADE YOU.

LUCY! STOP!

NOT ANOTHER WORD, LUCY. YOU'LL JUST MAKE THINGS WORSE.

WORSE?

it gets worse?

I HAVE NO MEMORIES OF ANYTHING BEFORE WE LEFT COLEOPOLIS.

RIP

JUST BE PATIENT. YOUR MEMORIES SHOULD **THEORETICALLY** RETURN.

eventually.

why didn't i notice this amnesia before...?

IT'S PART OF YOUR PROGRAMMING, DEAR.

RiiiGHT. BECAUSE I'M A **ROBOT.**

NO! YOU ARE SO MUCH **MORE** THAN THAT!

RIP

REALLY? DO TELL.

I... CAN'T.

RIP

uh... we have a situation here, folks.

TELL ME.

WE CAN'T, RAEF.

Y'KNOW, THIS IS ALL VERY INTERESTING, BUT THE BAG IS RIPPING AND WE NEED TO GET FREE SO THAT WE CAN FLY TO SAFETY!!!

THE LAST TIME I ANSWERED YOUR QUESTIONS, YOUR ENTIRE SYSTEM SHUT DOWN.

SO **REBOOT** ME!

IT'S NOT THAT SIMPLE.

WHY **NOT?**

BECAUSE YOU HAVE A **LIVING** BEETLE BRAIN.

I...

...what...?

R...

NO ONE **EVER** LISTENS TO ME.

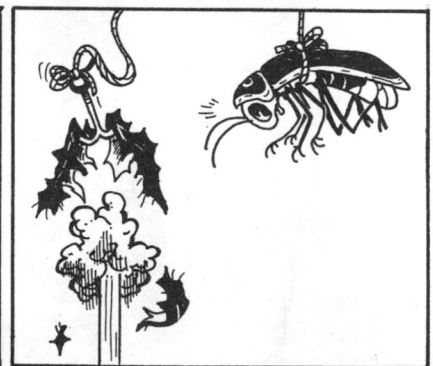

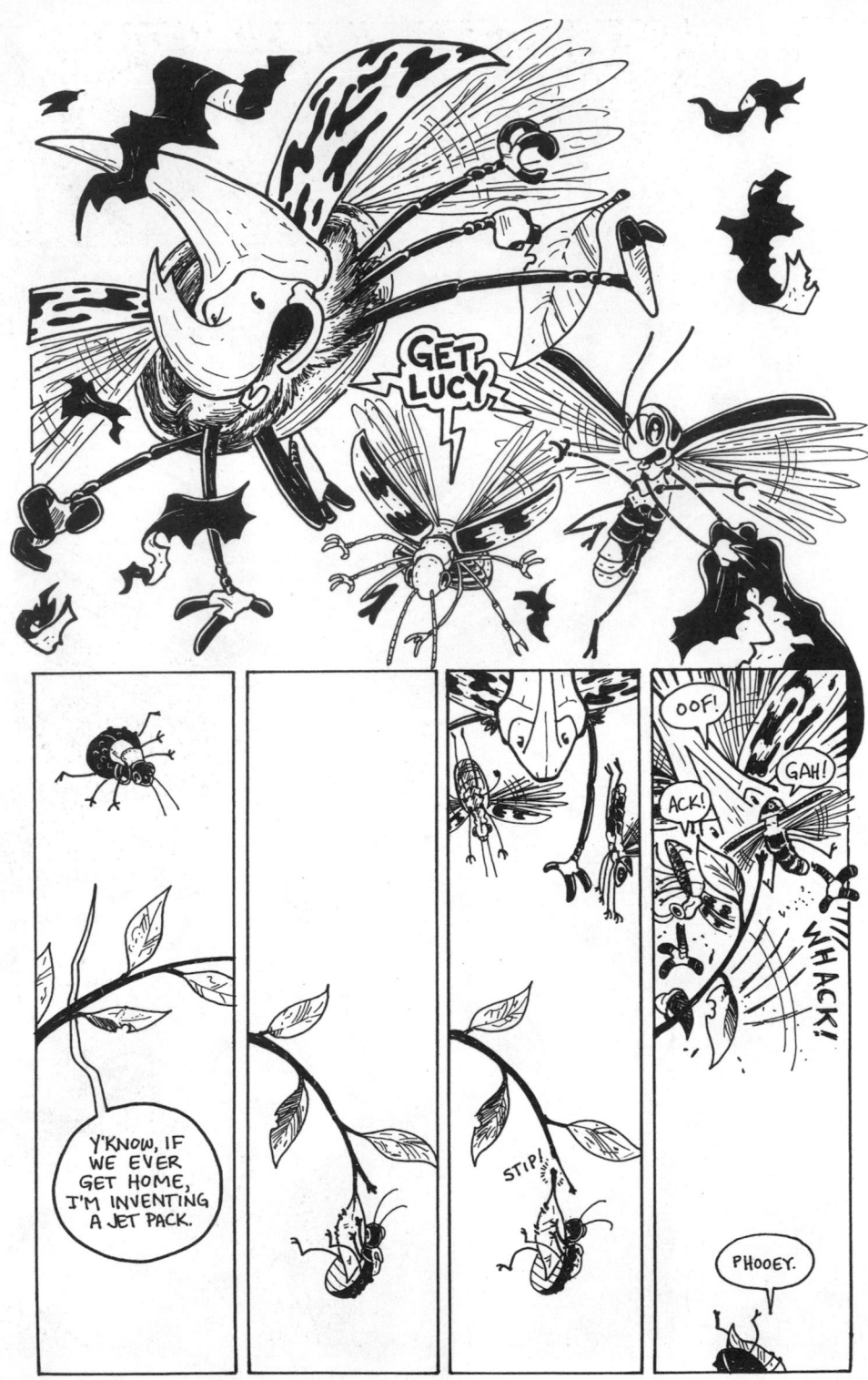

OWEN HAS IT.

OWEN DOES **NOT** HAVE MY NOTEBOOK.

YES, HE **DOES**. HE HAD IT WITH HIM RIGHT BEFORE HE ACTIVATED MY ROCKETS AND SENT US FLYING.

GIVE ME YOUR LEFT HAND.

WHY?

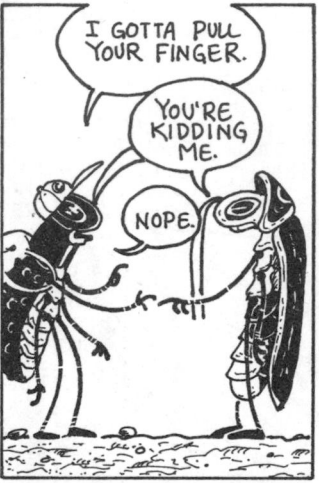

I GOTTA PULL YOUR FINGER.

YOU'RE KIDDING ME.

NOPE.

Sigh.

!!POP!!

PLUNK!

THIS ROBOT BODY COMES WITH EVERYTHING BUT **DIGNITY**, DOESN'T IT?

IT HAD TO BE SOMEWHERE OWEN WOULDN'T LOOK.

LOOK, SEE? MY NOTES ON THE SAND GIANT.

WELL, THAT'S A RELIEF, DEAR. BUT WHAT DOES THAT BEASTLY OWEN HAVE?

PROFESSOR OWEN! PROFESSOR OWEN!

WHAT **IS** IT, CAPTAIN?

I THINK YOU GAVE ME THE WRONG BOOK.

WHAT ARE YOU TALKING ABOUT?

I WENT TO ADD MY NOTES IN THE JOURNAL JUST AS YOU INSTRUCTED, BUT THERE'S NOTHING IN HERE EXCEPT THIS STRANGE NOTE.

LET ME SEE THAT!

DEAR DR. OWEN, I KNEW YOU COULDN'T BE TRUSTED.

I DON'T KNOW WHAT YOU'VE DONE, BUT IF YOU'RE READING THIS, THEN IT ISN'T GOOD.

IF I HAD TO GUESS, I'D SAY THERE'S A GOOD CHANCE WE'RE DEAD (IN WHICH CASE THERE ISN'T MUCH I CAN DO).

BUT, IF WE'RE ALIVE SOMEWHERE, ANYWHERE, YOU CAN REST ASSURED OF ONE THING:

Chapter 5

THAT SOUNDS LIKE MY CUE.

PROFESSOR!

I'VE GOT THIS ONE, RAEF.

YOU GET MOSSY.

WHEW! I DON'T THINK I COULD SURVIVE A DROP **THIS** HIGH.

HMPH. I **SHOULD** LET YOU TEST THAT.

DON'T YOU **EVER** LEAVE ME BEHIND **AGAIN**, DO YOU UNDERSTAND ME?

I WAS JUST—

EVER. AGAIN.

yes, ma'am, sorry.

GAH!

WE SURE DO SPEND A LOT OF TIME FALLING.

INCOMING!

TiNK!

ARE YOU GUYS OKAY?

wha...? what happened?

why can't i **see** anything..?

OH, MY GOSH! He's BLIND!

WOULD YOU GET **DOWN** FROM THERE?

HOW DO YOU FEEL, DEAR?

...all right, i guess..

THAT BIG, WEIRD -**THING**- REALLY KNOCKED YOU AROUND, MOSS.

FOR YOUR INFORMATION, THAT "THING"—AS YOU So **STUPIDLY** PUT IT—IS A DYNA-SOAR.

DUMB!

CLUELESS!

FUNNY LOOKIN'!

THERE'S NO NEED TO BE **RUDE**. WE'RE NOT FROM AROUND HERE.

YEAH? WELL, **RUDE** IS THE **LEAST** OF YOUR WORRIES. WHEN YOU TUMBLE ONTO OUR TURF, YOU TUMBLE INTO **TROUBLE**.

GRRR!

DON'T **MESS** WITH US.

WOOF! WOOF!

GRRR.

OKEY-DOKEY. LET'S GO BEFORE PEE-WEE HERE TAUNTS US TO DEATH.

I'D LOVE TO, BUT I'M NOT GOING ANYWHERE.

I'M STUCK.

Panel 1:

THERE'S SOMETHING STICKY ON THIS TREE AND I'M GLUED TIGHT.

THAT WOULD BE THE RESIN.

DID YOU LITTLE CREEPS PUT THIS HERE?

KINDA.

WHEN WE DRILL INTO THE BARK TO LAY OUR EGGS...

THE TREE TRIES TO GET RID OF US BY SECRETING STICKY RESIN.

IT'S LIKE THE TREE IS WEEPING.

THE BIG BABY.

Panel 2:

TOO BAD IT DOESN'T WORK BETTER.

YEAH, WELL, WHAT CAN WE SAY?

WE BAD!

WOOF!

WOOF!

WOOF!

WOOF!

Panel 3:

WHEN THE SMELL OF THE RESIN MIXES WITH ODORS WE RELEASE, IT MAKES A PERFUME THAT ATTRACTS MORE BEETLES LIKE US.

EVENTUALLY, OUR SUPERIOR NUMBERS OVERWHELM THE TREE'S DEFENSES.

IT DOESN'T STAND A CHANCE.

WE CAME AS SOON AS WE SMELLED.

GET OFF ME!

MAYBE WE CAN PRY YOU LOOSE.

GIVE IT A TRY.

YOU CAN'T GET OUT OF THE RESIN.

NOBODY GETS OUT OF THE RESIN.

FIRST TIME FOR EVERYTHING, SHORTY.

OUCH! OUCH! OUCH STOP!

YOU'RE RIPPING MY ELYTRA OFF!

TOLD YA.

HE'S A GONER.

WHAT IS THIS STUFF?

THE SCENT IS VAGUELY FAMILIAR.

IT'S RESIN!

THEY DON'T LISTEN.

IJITS

I WAS THINKING THE SAME THING.

WHERE HAVE I SMELLED...

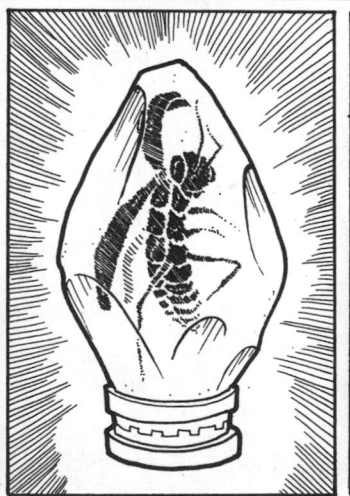

the amber beetle...

MY WORD, I THINK YOU'RE RIGHT.

MAYBE YOU'RE **STUCK** BECAUSE YOU'VE BEEN A NAUGHTY, NAUGHTY BEETLE, MOSSY.

ha ha

I DON'T GET IT. WHAT'S THE JOKE?

CAN WE TELL HIM? HE'S NOT IN THE STORY...

I SUPPOSE... AS LONG AS HE DOESN'T LEARN ANYTHING ABOUT HIMSELF THAT'LL MAKE HIM SHUT DOWN.

OKAY.

THE AMBER BEETLE IS AN ARTIFACT ON DISPLAY IN THE TEMPLE OF SCARABUS.

"WHEN I WAS A GRUB, OUR NURSERY WENT ON A FIELD TRIP TO VISIT IT."

...AND HERE WE HAVE THE AMBER BEETLE. AS YOU KNOW, ALMIGHTY SCARABUS STUCK THIS SINISTER BEETLE IN CLEAR GOLD, ONE THOUSAND YEARS AGO DURING THE FALL OF OLD COLEOPOLIS. IT REMAINS A WARNING TO US ALL:

"BE GOOD OR YOU'LL GET STUCK, TOO."

I COULDN'T ACTUALLY **SEE** THE AMBER BEETLE BECAUSE, WELL, GRUBS HAVE LOUSY EYES, BUT I COULD **IMAGINE** IT AND IT MADE ME SAD. BEING TRAPPED FOREVER SEEMED LIKE A **GHASTLY** PUNISHMENT. FOR WEEKS AFTERWARD, I DAYDREAMED OF SETTING IT FREE.

AFTER METAMORPHOSIS, I TOOK A JUNIOR FACULTY POSITION IN PROFESSOR BOMBARDIER'S LAB AND THE AMBER BEETLE CAUGHT MY ATTENTION AGAIN.

HAS ANYONE EVER ANALYZED THIS AMBER STUFF?

NOT THAT I KNOW OF.

AMBER BEETLE RESTORATION COMPLETE

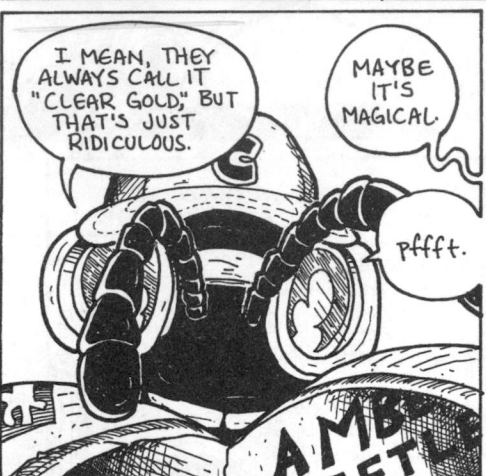

I MEAN, THEY ALWAYS CALL IT "CLEAR GOLD," BUT THAT'S JUST RIDICULOUS.

MAYBE IT'S MAGICAL.

pffft.

AMB ET

THE PROFESSOR SUGGESTED WE GO TO THE TEMPLE DIRECTOR AND ASK FOR A SAMPLE.

ABSOLUTELY NOT.

I UNDERSTAND.

THANK YOU FOR YOUR TIME.

DIRECTOR

THAT'S IT?

WELL, WHAT DO YOU WANT ME TO—

WHOOOPS!

TRIP!

oof!

BAM!

CLANK!

HEY! ARE YOU NUTS? WE JUST HAD THAT RESTORED!

...and you did a lovely job...

you really did...

OUT.

I am VERY sorry.

OUT!

ARE YOU OKAY?

NEVER BETTER.

I SCRAPED OFF A COUPLE FLAKES.

HUH..?

YOU ARE SO BAD.

TURNS OUT GETTING THE SAMPLE WAS THE EASY PART. THE ANALYSIS WAS A BIT MORE PROBLEMATIC.

I HAVE THE RESULTS.

AND?

THE AMBER IS MADE OF TERPENES.

THOSE ARE PLANT CHEMICALS.

NOT QUITE THE MYSTICAL MATERIAL THEY CLAIM, EH, DEAR?

TIC TAC TAC TAC TIC TIC TAC

THERE'S MORE. THESE TERPENES AREN'T FROM ANY PLANTS FOUND IN THE OASIS.

OH, MY. **THAT'S** INTERESTING.

I THOUGHT SO, TOO.

I FIGURED THE TERPENES MIGHT BE FROM SOME UNKNOWN PLANT THAT LIVED DURING THE FALL OF OLD COLEOPOLIS, SO I USED DR. LIBBY'S EXPERIMENTAL RADIOACTIVE DATING DEVICE TO SEE IF THE FLAKE WAS ACTUALLY A THOUSAND YEARS OLD.

IS IT?

NO, MA'AM. IT'S OLDER.

HOW **MANY** YEARS OLDER?

MILLIONS.

♪

YOU'VE CHECKED THE CALCULATIONS?

FOUR TIMES. **WITH** PROFESSOR LIBBY.

WELL, LET'S RUN IT AGAIN WITH THE SECOND FLAKE.

DID YOU GET THE SAME RESULTS?

WE DIDN'T GET **ANY** RESULTS. THE SECOND FLAKE DISAPPEARED BEFORE WE COULD REPEAT THE TEST.

YEAH... HEH... TOTALLY WEIRD, HUH?

STILL, WE HAD ENOUGH DATA TO PRESENT AT THE MONTHLY MEETING OF THE ROYAL SOCIETY FOR SCIENCE.

that went well...

...IN CONCLUSION, I BELIEVE THE AMBER'S EXTREME AGE AND UNKNOWN PLANT SOURCE SUGGEST THE WORLD IS A FAR MORE MYSTERIOUS PLACE THAN WE HAD PREVIOUSLY THOUGHT.

THANK YOU FOR YOUR ATTENTION. ARE THERE ANY QUESTIONS?

YES. YOU SUGGEST GREATER MYSTERIES, BUT I THINK THE EXPLANATION FOR YOUR "EXTREME AGE" MEASUREMENTS IS ANYTHING **BUT** MYSTERIOUS. YOU USED A NEW, EXPERIMENTAL TECHNIQUE AND GOT THE WRONG ANSWER.

THAT'S **POSSIBLE**, SIR. HOWEVER, IT DOESN'T ADDRESS THE FACT THAT THE AMBER CAME FROM A COMPLETELY UNKNOWN PLANT.

CLEARLY, IT IS FROM ONE OF THE MANY INIQUITOUS PLANTS THAT SCARABUS EXPUNGED FROM THE OASIS DURING THE FALL OF OLD COLEOPOLIS.

ARE YOU SERIOUSLY SUGGESTING THE AMBER IS FROM **EVIL** PLANTS?

THE WICKED TAKE MANY FORMS.

BUT... THAT'S JUST... SILLY.

THESE RESULTS SUGGEST THAT MANY OF OUR ASSUMPTIONS ABOUT THE WORLD COULD BE WRONG.

EARTH COULD BE INCREDIBLY OLD.

AND IT MIGHT CONTAIN STRANGE, UNDISCOVERED FORMS OF LIFE.

RUBBISH! THERE IS NO LIFE BEYOND THE OASIS.

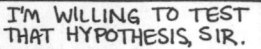

I'M WILLING TO TEST THAT HYPOTHESIS, SIR.

AS AM I.

AND HOW WOULD YOU DO **THAT**? LEAVE THE OASIS?

DON'T BE ABSURD.

WHY **NOT**? I'M NOT AFRAID OF WHAT WE MIGHT FIND.

ARE YOU?

IT WAS A VERY **PUBLIC** CHALLENGE OF THE MINISTER OF SCIENCE.

AND BY THAT SHE MEANS A VERY **STUPID, HOT-HEADED** PUBLIC CHALLENGE.

Panel 1:
WELL, THAT EXPLAINS WHY HE HATES US...

NAH. IT GOES MUCH DEEPER THAN THAT.

Panel 2:
THERE WAS ENOUGH PRESSURE FROM A FEW OF THE ROYAL SOCIETY'S SENIOR SCIENTISTS THAT OWEN WAS COMPELLED TO GIVE US **SOME** FUNDING, BUT IT WASN'T MUCH.

HENCE, THE EMBARRASSING BURLAP BACKPACK I WAS CARRYING OUR SUPPLIES IN.

... AND HE INSISTED ON COMING ALONG TO SUPERVISE.

Panel 3:
DO YOU HAVE ANY IDEA WHAT THEY'RE TALKING ABOUT?

ABOUT TEN MINUTES TOO LONG, I'D SAY.

HA! NICE ONE.

WOOF!

WOOF!

WOOF!

Panel 4:
WHY DO YOU GUYS KEEP MAKING THAT SOUND?

WE LIVE IN TREE BARK.

IT'S A PUN.

OOOOII, I LOVE PUNS.

Panel 5:
WE'RE BARKING.

LIKE A DOG.

uh huh.

'CAUSE WE'RE **BARK** BEETLES.

Ahhn.

Panel 6:
WHAT'S A DOG?

ARE YOU KIDDING?

LISTEN, BRAINLESS, IF YOU DON'T—

Panel 7:
CHK-RIEEEEEP!

gulp!

gotta go.

CHK-REEEEEP!

GET AWAY FROM THEM!

BAZZAP!

Yikes, what was that...?

IT WAS AWESOME! DO IT AGAIN!

I'LL TRY.

FEEL MY PIERCING GAZE!

CLICK

huh.

GUESS I'M STILL A LONG WAY FROM UNDERSTANDING THIS ROBOT BODY.

WHAT HAPPENED?

I'M NOT SURE, BUT I THINK I JUST TOOK A PICTURE.

OH, WELL, BABY STEPS.

ONE BLAST WAS MORE THAN ENOUGH.

THE IMPORTANT THING IS THAT WE FREED MOSSY AND VANQUISHED THE DYNA-SOAR!

IT'S ALL VERY EXCITING, DEAR.

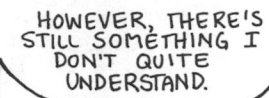

HOWEVER, THERE'S STILL SOMETHING I DON'T QUITE UNDERSTAND.

HOW DID YOU KNOW THE AMYL ALCOHOL SOLUTION WOULD WORK?

I JUST FIGURED SINCE THEY WERE MADE OF SIMILAR TERPENES, THAT SOMETHING THAT DISSOLVES AMBER WOULD DISSOLVE THE RESIN.

MAKES SENSE.

BUT HOW DID YOU KNOW WHAT WOULD DISSOLVE AMBER?

Oh... THAT...

I MENTIONED THAT THE AMBER BEETLE MADE ME SAD, DIDN'T I?

YOU DID.

I MEAN, IT REALLY AFFECTED ME.

YES.

DEEPLY.

LUCY...

SO, JUST IN CASE I EVER GOT A CHANCE TO, Y'KNOW, FREE IT, I...

...I sorta tested some chemicals on the second flake.

YOU DESTROYED THAT FLAKE?

YES, MA'AM.

AN INVALUABLE SCIENTIFIC SAMPLE?

Yes.

YOU...

Chapter 6

IT HAS BEEN TWO DAYS SINCE OUR RUN-IN WITH THE DYNA-SOAR AND THE REALITY OF OUR SITUATION HAS SUNK IN. EVERYBODY IS QUIET. RAEF FEELS PARTICULARLY BAD AFTER BLASTING A HOLE IN OUR LAST CANTEEN WITH HIS LASER EYE BEAMS.

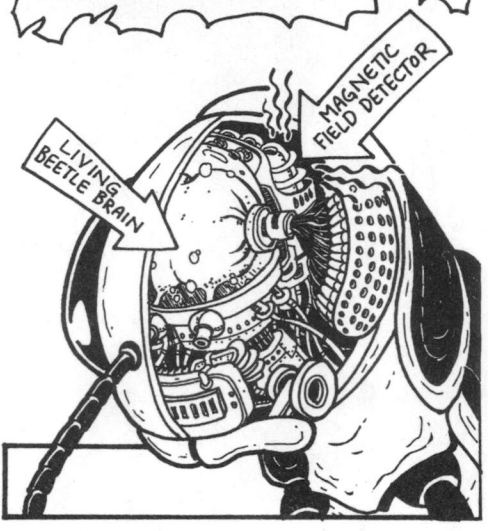

THE GOOD NEWS IS THAT HE HAS A BUILT-IN DEVICE THAT CAN DETECT THE EARTH'S MAGNETIC FIELD. BY COMPARING THE MAGNETIC FIELD OF OUR CURRENT LOCATION TO A RECORD OF THE MAGNETIC FIELD IN NEW COLEOPOLIS, WE'VE DETERMINED THAT HOME IS DUE EAST.

LIVING BEETLE BRAIN

MAGNETIC FIELD DETECTOR

THE BAD NEWS IS WE HAVE NO IDEA HOW FAR AWAY WE ARE.

LIKE I SAID, I **SHOULD** BE DEPRESSED.

BUT I'M NOT.

BACK HOME ALL WE HAVE ARE BEETLES, A FEW DOMESTICATED MOTHS, AND A HANDFUL OF OTHER CRITTERS. BUT THIS PLACE IS OVERRUN WITH BIZARRE NEW LIFE-FORMS. I KINDA FEEL LIKE I JUST WOKE UP FROM A REALLY BORING BLACK-AND-WHITE DREAM TO FIND A WORLD FULL OF CRAZY COLORS.

DON'T GET ME WRONG. NO ONE WANTS TO GET HOME AND WRAP THEIR FINGERS AROUND OWEN'S SCRAWNY LITTLE NECK MORE THAN ME.

I JUST WANT TO GO SLOWLY.

VERY SLOWLY.

I DON'T WANT THE WONDER TO STOP. EACH EXOTIC NEW THING ADDS TO THE MYSTERY OF THIS PLACE.

AND I **LOVE** A GOOD MYSTERY.

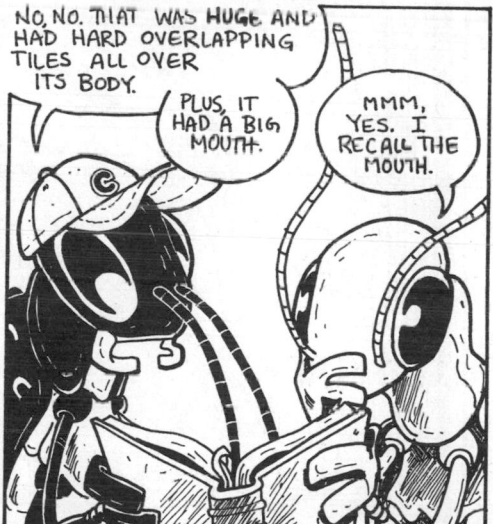

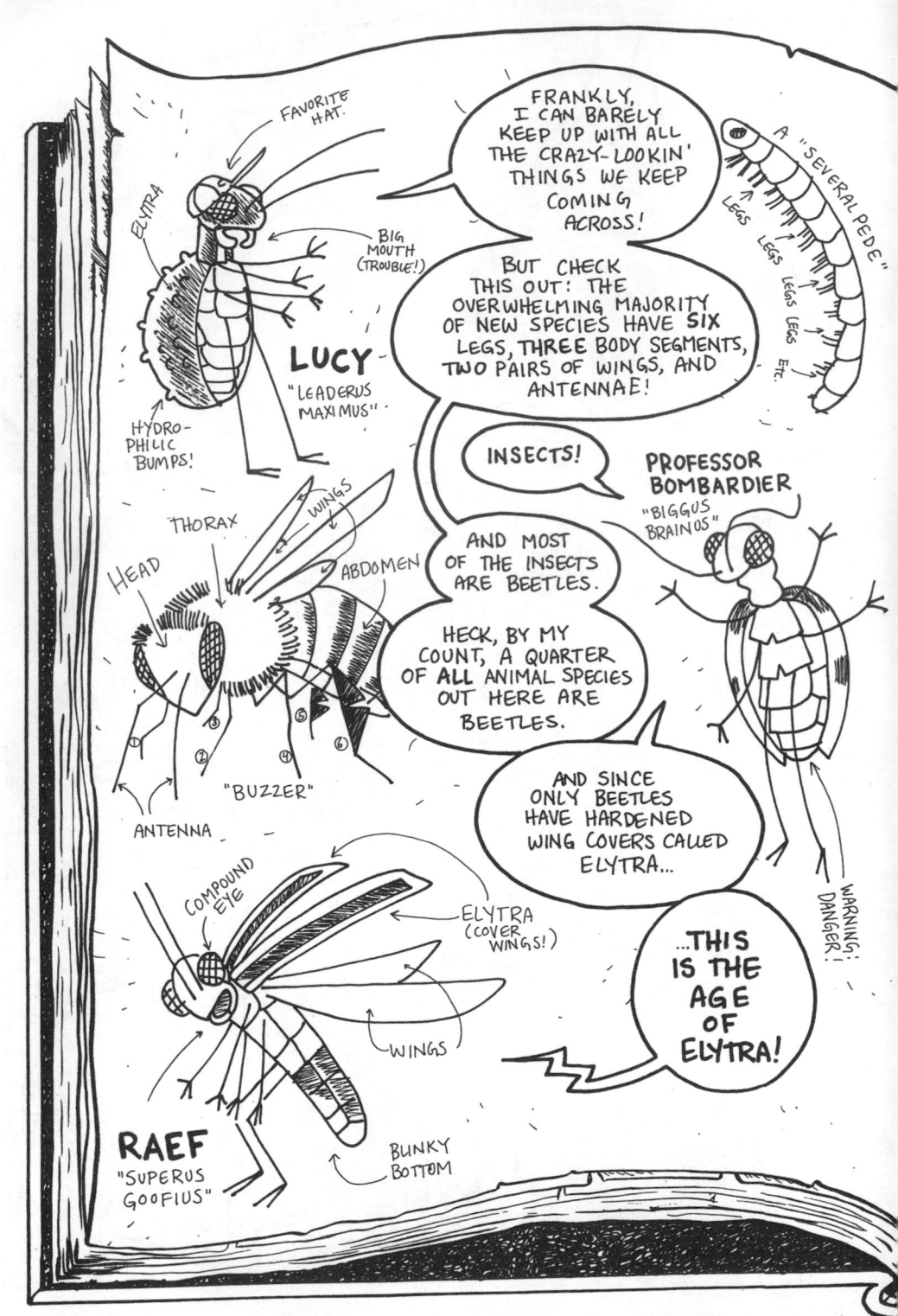

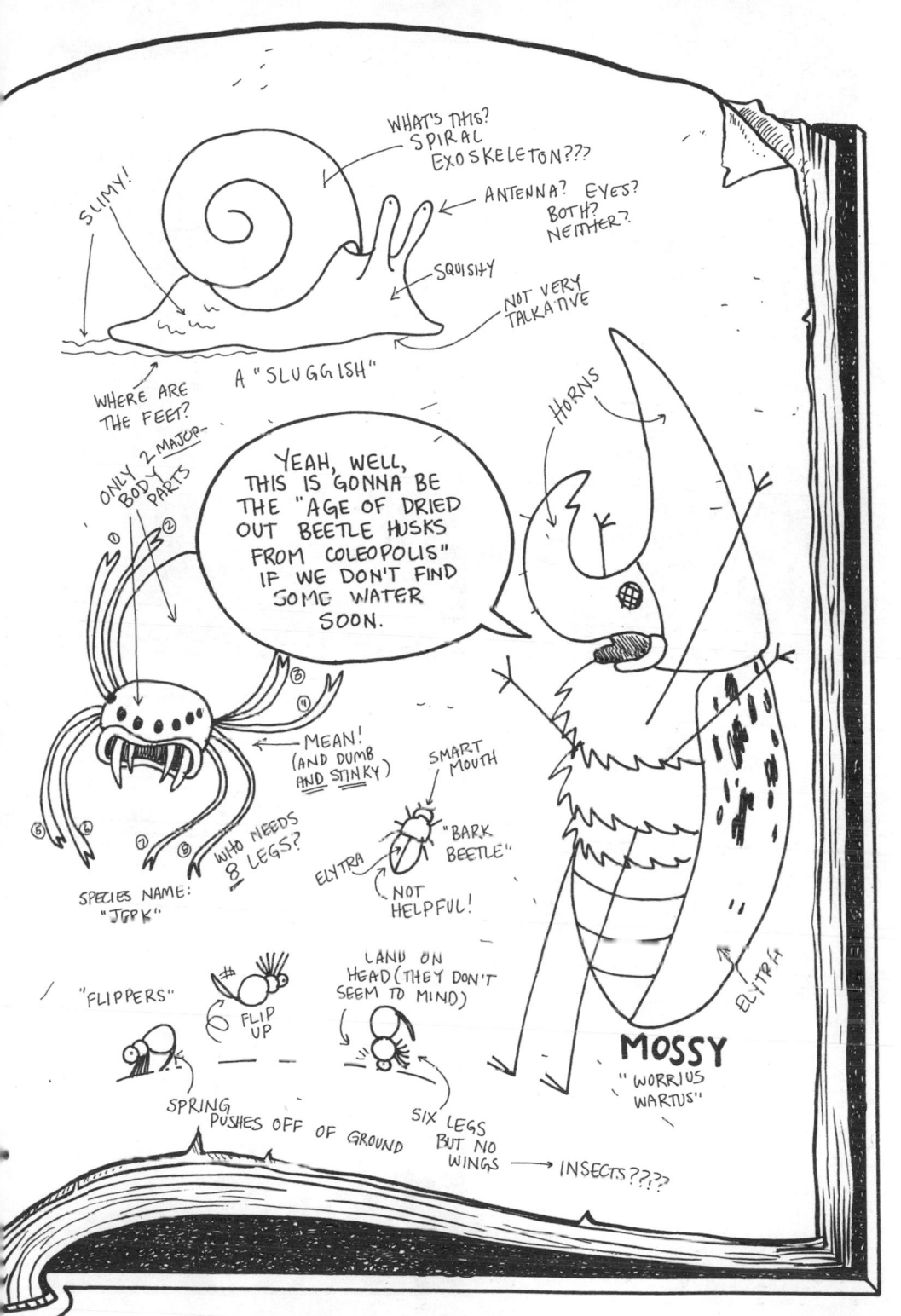

MOSSY'S RIGHT. WE NEED TO ORGANIZE A SEARCH.

WE'LL FORM TWO GROUPS.

YOU TWO GO THAT WAY. RAEF AND I WILL LOOK IN THE OPPOSITE DIRECTION.

YOU AND RAEF ALONE?

I'M NOT SURE THAT'S THE BEST...

...uh...

RIGHT.

good teams.

BUT WE'RE NOT GOING TO LOOK FOR LONG, OKAY? IT'LL BE DARK SOON.

AGREED.

Panel 1:

WE'LL SET UP THE ODOR BEACON AND MEET BACK HERE.

Panel 2:

BE CAREFUL!

YOU, TOO.

Panel 3:

WOW. SHE GAVE YOU THE LOOK.

YEAH, THOSE ARE USUALLY RESERVED FOR YOU.

WELL, I AM THE IDIOT ON THIS TEAM.

TOO BAD FOR US YOU'RE ALSO THE ONE IN CHARGE.

Panel 4:

YEP. WHO ELSE BUT AN IDIOT WOULD HAVE LED US INTO THIS MESS?

OH, GIMME A BREAK.

IF I HADN'T TAUNTED OWEN IN THE DESERT, HE WOULDN'T HAVE TURNED ON US AND WE WOULD BE HOME RIGHT NOW BASKING IN THE SCIENTIFIC GLORY OF THAT GIANT THING WE FOUND.

PFFT!

OWEN HAD THIS PLANNED ALL ALONG. THAT FINK WOULD HAVE TURNED ON US EVEN IF YOU HAD BEEN ON YOUR BEST BEHAVIOR.

AND NOW HE'S TAKING CREDIT FOR OUR DISCOVERY.

SHH! YOU HEAR THAT?

SOUNDS LIKE SOMEONE SCRAPING A STICK AGAINST A FILE.

WHATEVER IT IS, IT'S ANNOYING.

ZZZT ZZZT ZZZT ZZZT

HEY! WE HEAR YOU, OKAY?

NOW WOULD YOU PLEASE SHUT-OOOOOP!!

EEEE! ZZZT ZZZZZT ZZZT ZZZZT ZZZZT ZZT LUCY!

WHOA... DID YOU HEAR THAT?

HEAR WHAT, DEAR?

HMMM. IT'S GONE NOW.

I GUESS THE DARK IS MAKING ME KINDA JUMPY.

WHY DON'T YOU TURN ON YOUR LIGHT?

IS THAT A GOOD IDEA?

WE DON'T KNOW HOW LONG IT WILL TAKE TO GET HOME. I DON'T WANT TO WEAR OUT THE BULB.

DO WE HAVE AN EXTRA?

THERE'S NO BULB, DEAR.

YOU MAKE LIGHT THE SAME WAY ALL FIREFLIES DO.

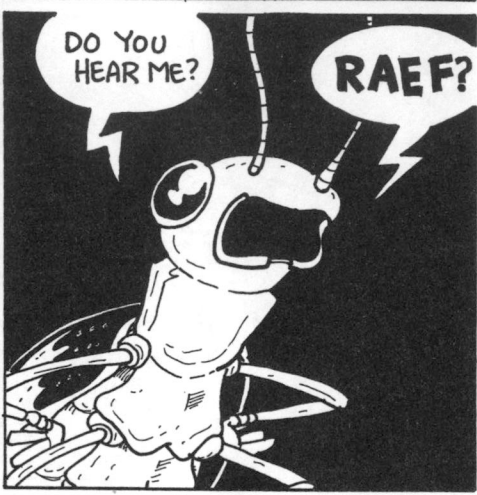

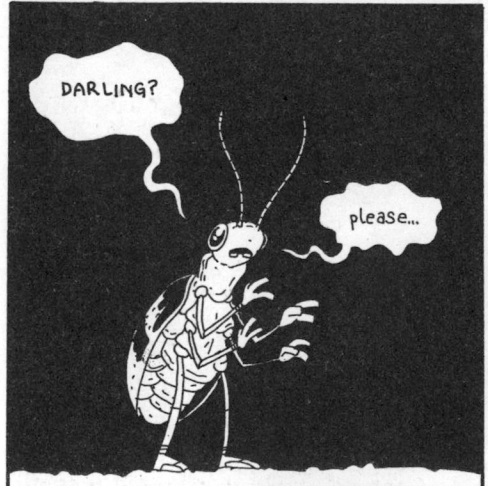

Chapter 7

LUCY?
MOSSY, REMEMBER THE DESERT GIANT WE FOUND?
OF COURSE.
REMEMBER THE PART THAT LOOKED LIKE A CAGE?
YES, BUT WHAT DOES THAT—
I THINK I JUST HIT MY HAND ON ANOTHER ONE...
WAAA! MOMMA, MAKE THE BAD BEETLE GO AWAY!
ZZT
ZZZZT
ZZZZT
I'M SCRAPING AS HARD AS I CAN, DEAR.
LOOK, I'M GOIN', BUT CAN YOU TELL ME WHERE I CAN FIND MORE OF THESE?
BABIES? WELL, THE WILSONS JUST HAD A BROOD AND I HEAR THEY LOOK MUCH YUMMIER THAN OURS.
NOT THE GRUBS, YOU GHOUL, THESE HARD THINGS!
BONES? THERE'S THE OLD ABANDONED JONES PLACE.
OH, YES! THEY HAD A MUCH BIGGER MOUSE.
Yeah, and he let me know that every chance he got.
IT'S NOT A COMPETITION, DEAR.
CAN YOU SHOW ME?

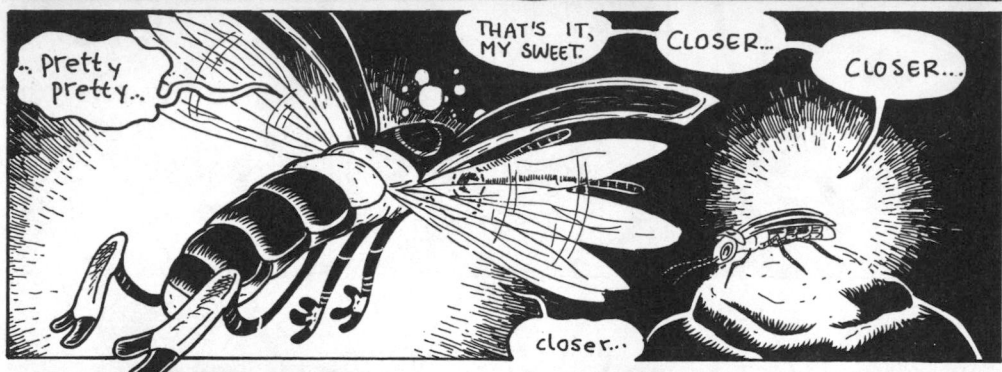

SADLY, TWINKLE'S SPECIES DOESN'T EAT THE SAME FOOD AND THAT MAKES ME FEEL SO VULNERABLE. BUT WHEN **YOU** BECOME ONE WITH MY DIGESTIVE TRACT, I WILL EXTRACT AND STORE YOUR LOVELY TOXINS IN MY BODY AND EGGS.

YOUR ESSENCE WILL HELP PROTECT ME AND MY EGGS FROM THE HORRIBLE, HORRIBLE WORLD.

ISN'T THAT ROMANTIC? I JUST— **AH!**

oh, great.

BZZT!

BOING!

NOW LOOK WHAT YOU'VE DONE!

I CAN'T BREAK YOUR CUTICLE!

OH, DARLING, WHY MUST YOU ALWAYS KEEP ME OUT?

CAN'T YOU SEE IT'S KILLING ME?

KILLING YOU?

GIVE ME YOUR POISON!

WELL, YOU BRAZEN SIREN, IF YOU WANTED TO SHARE NASTY TOXIC CHEMICALS, WHY DIDN'T YOU SAY SO?

I AM MORE THAN HAPPY TO OBLIGE.

MEANWHILE...

SO YOU GUYS BURY THOSE HUGE DEAD ANIMALS ALL BY YOURSELF?

YEP. IT'S A LOT OF WORK, BUT I GOTTA FEED MY BABIES.

OH, HEY, THERE'S BOB. 'SCUSE ME A SEC.

HEY, BOB, WHATCHA GOT?

FIELD MOUSE. unh.

JUST SHIFTIN' IT TO A BETTER BURIAL SPOT.

MAY I SEE?

OKAY BY ME.

I NEED A BREAK.

IT'S SOFT ON THE OUTSIDE JUST LIKE THE DYNA-SOAR. AND IT HAS HAIRS ALL OVER.

YEAH, WHAT A PAIN. WE GOTTA SKIN IT BEFORE WE CAN USE IT.

ELSEWHERE...

IS THAT HOW YOU ESCAPED FROM THE MOUTH OF THAT BEASTIE IN THE DESERT?

IT IS.

WOW. YOU'RE LIKE SOME KIND OF... SUPER BEETLE!

IF YOU SAY SO, DEAR. ARE YOU OKAY?

YEAH, JUST A LITTLE CONFUSED. I HAVE NO IDEA HOW I GOT HERE.

I THINK THAT... AWFUL BEETLE... WAS MIMICKING THE PULSES OF YOUR SPECIES' NATURAL MATING SIGNAL. YOU WERE INSTINCTIVELY DRAWN TO IT.

IT REALLY STINGS!

huh. WELL, I MAY BE A ROBOT, BUT IT'S NICE TO KNOW THE PART OF MY BRAIN IN CHARGE OF LOVE STILL WORKS.

YES...

Yes, it is...

AHEM! IN ANY EVENT, WE SHOULD FIND THE OTHERS AND HAVE LUCY TAKE A LOOK AT YOU.

GOOD IDEA. MAYBE SHE CAN HELP ME GET MY HEAD SCREWED ON STRAIGHT.

ugh. YOU AND YOUR PUNS.

LATER...

...SO, AT FIRST I HAD NO IDEA WHAT THAT DESERT GIANT MIGHT BE, BUT AFTER SEEING THOSE MOUSE "BONES" I THINK THE GIANT MIGHT BE **THE INTERNAL** SKELETON OF SOME GINORMOUS MOUSE-LIKE CREATURE.

I DID A PRELIMINARY SKETCH BASED ON MY NOTES.

SEE?

FASCINATING.

DESERT GIANT PR-----NA----- SKETCH.

head may be a bit off

upright or all fours?

DIDN'T SEE TAIL & BONES MISSING!

"HAIR"

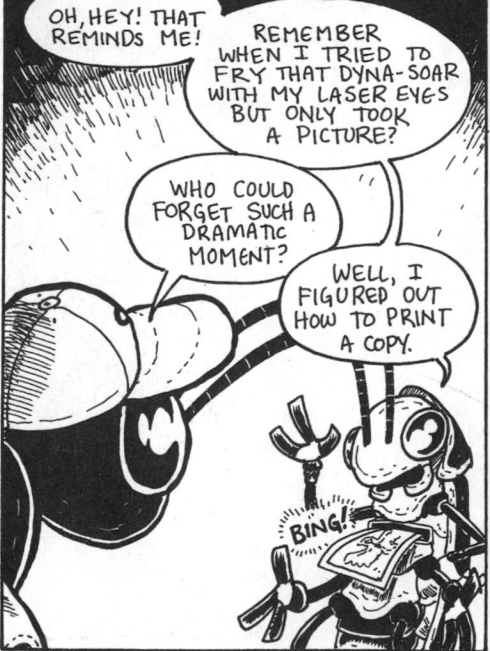

OH, HEY! THAT REMINDS ME!

REMEMBER WHEN I TRIED TO FRY THAT DYNA-SOAR WITH MY LASER EYES BUT ONLY TOOK A PICTURE?

WHO COULD FORGET SUCH A DRAMATIC MOMENT?

WELL, I FIGURED OUT HOW TO PRINT A COPY.

BING!

oh, my!

YOU ACTIVATED THE **EXPERIMENTAL** PROGRAM FOR TAKING INTEGRATED SONO-ELECTROMAGNETIC REFLECTANCE/ PENETRATION SCANS.

I'M SO SORRY!

I DIDN'T KNOW WHAT I WAS DOING!

NO, NO, IT'S **GREAT!** IT INTEGRATES ULTRASONIC WAVES AND INFRARED RADIATION TO GENERATE AN IMAGE LIKE AN X-RAY.

OH, IN THAT CASE, I MEANT TO DO THAT.

LOOK AT **THIS.** EVEN THOUGH A MOUSE AND DYNA-SOAR LOOK VERY **DIFFERENT,** THEIR SKELETONS LOOK VERY **SIMILAR.**

SOUNDS LIKE A FASCINATING THING TO CONSIDER, LUCY.

AT ANOTHER TIME.

FIRST THINGS FIRST.

YOU GUYS DIDN'T FIND ANY WATER EITHER?

I'M AFRAID NOT, DEAR.

THEN I SUGGEST WE TRAVEL AT NIGHT TO AVOID THE HEAT OF DAY UNTIL WE FIND SOME.

A VERY SENSIBLE NOTION, YOU BIG BLUNDERING BEHEMOTH.

EXCEPT FOR ONE THING.

Chapter 8

LOOK, I DON'T KNOW WHO YOU ARE, OLD-TIMER, BUT DON'T THREATEN US.

WE'VE HAD A **BAD** NIGHT.

S'NOT A THREAT. LOOK AT YER FEET. SEE THE SILK STRANDS SPARKLIN' IN THE FIREFLY'S GLOW?

silk...?

NO, IT'S THE **SANDWALKER** I MEAN TO TALK TO.

sandwalker?

YOU WANT MY HELP?

GAH! OF COURSE WE DO!

TAKE ME WITH YOU BACK TO COLEOPOLIS.

FINE. GREAT. WHATEVER. **JUST GET ON WITH IT!**

EXCELLENT. TELL YOUR BURLY SERVANT TO ROLL THAT ROCK OVER THE TRAPDOOR FLAP.

MOSSY, YOU NEED TO—

I HEARD HIM!

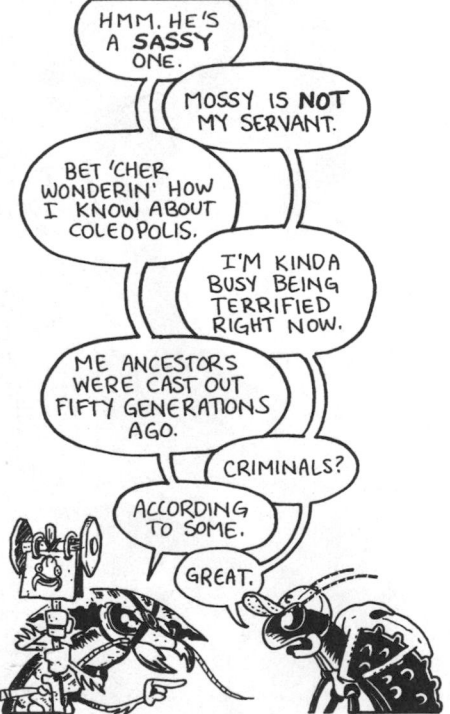

HMM. HE'S A **SASSY** ONE.

MOSSY IS **NOT** MY SERVANT.

BET 'CHER WONDERIN' HOW I KNOW ABOUT COLEOPOLIS.

I'M KINDA BUSY BEING TERRIFIED RIGHT NOW.

ME ANCESTORS WERE CAST OUT FIFTY GENERATIONS AGO.

CRIMINALS?

ACCORDING TO SOME.

GREAT.

I COULD USE A HAND HERE, GRAMPS.

DO I **LOOK** LIKE A COMMON LABORER?

RAZZA RAZZA

HE LOST THEM ANTENNAE PROTECTING YOU, D'INT HE?

HOW COULD YOU KNOW THAT?

I KNOW THE OLD STORIES. SANDWALKERS WERE CAST OUT LONG BEFORE MY PEOPLE.

WHAT ARE YOU TALKING ABOUT?

rrrrrr

BET YOU WERE ONE OF A KIND IN COLEOPOLIS. **DIFFERENT.** PICKED ON A BIT, MAYBE?

hmph, more than a bit.

RRRRRR

ALWAYS FEELIN' LIKE YOU HAD TO **PROVE** YOURSELF.

PRETTY SURE I DON'T LIKE YOU, OLD-TIMER.

RRRRRRRR

HEE-YAA!

WHUMP!

?

MOVE!

I'M CLEAR.

RAEF, GET LUCY.

I'M ON IT!

TWANNG!

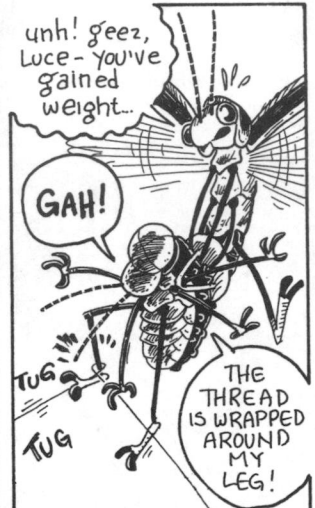

unh! geez, Luce - you've gained weight...

GAH!

THE THREAD IS WRAPPED AROUND MY LEG!

TUG
TUG
TUG

HARD TO REACH!

TUG
TUG
TUG
TUG

WOULD YOU **PLEASE** STOP TUGGING ON THAT— ACK!

TUG
TUG

BWA-HA-HAAAA!

PEEK-A-BOO, I EAT Y—

what the heck?

GET BACK IN THERE!

wha...?

WHAT'S ON MY TRAPDOOR?

GOTTA STOP BUILDING YER TRAP SO CLOSE TO BIG ROCKS, MORLOCK.

MA'DOG! ALWAYS MESSING WITH ME.

WELL, YOU DID EAT ME LEG.

YESSS, IT WAS TASTY...

FINE. YOU'VE TRAPPED ME...

... BUT I CAN STILL REACH.

HURRY UP!

I'M HURRY-UPPING AS FAST AS I CAN!

YOINK!

NO. NO. NO.

TWANG!

NO!

curse you, Ma'dog.

DON'T BE MAD, OLD FRIEND.

IF IT'S ANY CONSOLATION, I DIDN'T THINK THEY'D ACTUALLY MAKE IT.

I'LL GET OUT OF THIS, Y'KNOW.

YOU ALWAYS DO.

AND THEN I'M GONNA EAT YOU ALIVE!

NAH. BY THE TIME YOU'RE FREE, I'LL BE LOOOONG GONE, MORLOCK.

ME FRIENDS HERE ARE TAKING ME HOME.

friends?

MAYBE THE WORD MEANS SOMETHING DIFFERENT OUT HERE.

HEY, WHAT ARE WE? CHOPPED LARVAE?

THAT STILL DOESN'T EXPLAIN WHY THEY WERE EXILED, MA'DOG.

STORYTELLING ISN'T A CRIME.

TRUE, BUT A FEW KAMA-SHEEBAY LEARNED OF A SINISTER GROUP CALLED **THE ORDER OF THE SCARABI**. THE ORDER BELIEVED THEY WERE CHOSEN BY SCARABUS TO RULE OVER ALL OF COLEOPOLIS.

NATURALLY, ME ANCESTORS STARTED TO TELL EVERYONE. UNFORTUNATELY, THE SCARABI HAD POWERFUL ALLIES WHO CALLED THE KAMA-SHEEBAY BLASPHEMOUS TRAITORS AND HAD THEM CAST OUT OF THE OASIS.

MOST DIED TRYING TO CROSS THE DESERT, BUT A FEW WERE SAVED BY A SMALL BAND OF SANDWALKERS.

THAT'S WHEN ME ANCESTORS LEARNED THEY WEREN'T THE FIRST BEETLES TO BE TREATED SO ROUGHLY. THE SANDWALKERS HAD BEEN EXILED LONG BEFORE US.

BUT, WHY WERE—

AK!

TRIP!

YOU OKAY?

m'fine

REMIND ME AGAIN **WHY** WE'RE WALKING IN THE DARK AND NOT USING RAEF'S LIGHT TO GUIDE THE WAY?

HOW MANY TIMES I GOTTA SAY IT, GIRL?

WE DON'T NEED MR. BLINKY-BUTT ADVERTISING OUR PRESENCE TO EVERY PREDATOR LURKING IN THE SHADOWS.

RIGHT. LURKING IN THE SHADOWS LIKE THESE MYSTERIOUS "SCARABI"?

THE SCARABI ARE REAL ENOUGH.

YEAH? WELL, I'VE NEVER HEARD OF THEM AND I'VE ACTUALLY **BEEN** TO COLEOPOLIS.

JUST 'CAUSE **YOU** HAIN'T HEARD OF SOMETHIN' DON'T MEAN THAT IT ISN'T DANGEROUS.

BETCHA CAN'T HEAR THE **SCREAMERS** FLYIN' ALL AROUND US, BUT THEY COULD STILL KILL YA.

Screamers?

GREAT FURRY BEASTS.

HUNT AT NIGHT.

GOBBLE UP INSECTS.

Th-They can see... in the dark?

DON'T BE STUPID, THEY **HEAR** IN THE DARK. THEY FLY AROUND SCREAMING THEIR BLOODY HEADS OFF AND LISTENING FOR THE ECHOES TO BOUNCE OFF CRITTERS TO EAT.

oh, c'mon.

WHY DO YOU THINK WE'RE WALKIN' WHEN FLYIN' IS FASTER?

WELL, FOR ONE THING, I CAN'T FLY.

YEAH, WELL EVEN IF YOU COULD, WE WOULDN'T.

THERE ARE TWO SCREAMERS FLYIN' ABOVE US RIGHT NOW.

I DON'T HEAR ANYTHING.

THAT'S 'CAUSE THEY'RE SCREAMIN' HIGHER THAN YER WEE LITTLE EARS CAN HEAR.

Soooo, YOU'RE HEARING VOICES THAT ONLY YOUR MAGICAL EARS CAN PERCEIVE?

TAIN'T MAGIC! ALL OF ME SPECIES CAN HEAR THE SCREAMERS' CALLS.

IT TRIGGERS OUR ESCAPE BEHAVIOR.

AT THIS VERY MOMENT I'M FIGHTING THE URGE TO DROP TO THE GROUND AND SKITTER AWAY...

DON'T LET US STOP YOU.

I HEARD THA—

uh, buyum.

uh... what...

DON'T.

MOVE.

one more step...

...and we're dead.

YOU JUST **LOVE** SAYING THAT, DON'T YOU?

THAT'S A **VERY** BIG CATERPILLAR...

TAIN'T A CATERPILLAR.

IT'S A **VELVET** WORM.

I TAKE IT THEY AREN'T AS SNUGGLY AS THEIR NAME SUGGESTS?

STANDING HERE IS CRAZY!

AYE, BUT FLYIN' WOULD BE EVEN CRAZIER. SCREAMERS ARE SWARMING ABOVE US.

PERHAPS— =oop=

I AGREE.

EVERYONE CLIMB INTO MY ARMS. IF THERE'S TROUBLE, I'LL TAKE OFF.

BUT MAYBE WE SHOULD BE MORE CONCERNED WITH THE THREAT WE CAN ACTUALLY SEE.

STAND STILL, YOU SUICIDAL IJITS! YOU'LL GET US ALL KILLED!

WE ARE NOT GOING TO DIE ENCASED IN WORM SNOT BECAUSE SOME CRAZY OLD COOT IS AFRAID OF INVISIBLE SKY MONSTERS THAT HUNT USING SILENT SCREAMS.

THEM MONSTERS ARE REAL AND THEY EAT THEIR WEIGHT IN INSECTS EVERY NIGHT. THEY'LL ADD YOU TO THE MENU, IF YOU DON'T STAY PUT.

OH, YEAH? WELL, LET'S SEE JUST HOW "REAL" THESE MONSTERS ARE...

CHOMP!

GAH!

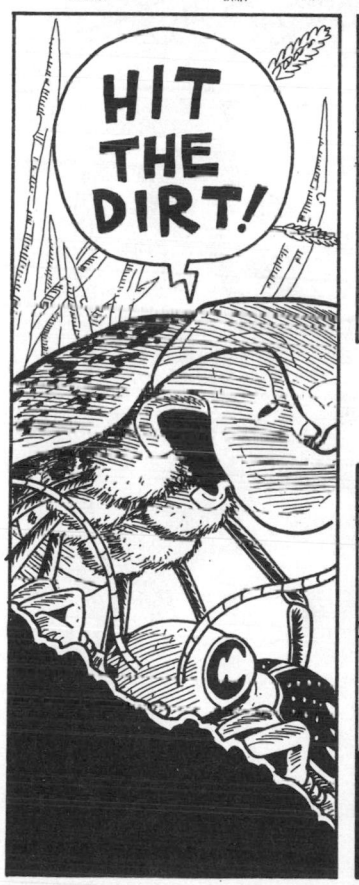

HIT THE DIRT!

GET DOWN, RAEF!

NO, WAIT!

LOOK OUT FOR THE VELVET— OOOF!

HEEELP US!

I'M COMING, RAEF.

NO.

IF YOU TOUCH US, YOU'LL GET STUCK, TOO.

LEAVE 'EM, WE GOTTA GET OUT OF HERE.

WE'RE NOT GOING ANYWHERE.

SOMEBODY **DO** SOMETHING!

gimme a sec, I'll figure something out.

YOU WOULDN'T HAVE TO FIGURE **ANYTHING** OUT IF YOU HADN'T TURNED ON MY LIGHT WITHOUT ASKING.

LET'S STAY FOCUSED, DEAR. I'LL TRY TO HOLD OFF THE VELVET WORMS.

AND I'LL MAKE SURE OUR "SCREAMER DETECTOR" DOESN'T RUN OFF.

WHAT? YA KIN'T HOLD ME AGAINST ME WILL!

I EITHER **HOLD** YOU OR **TOSS** YOU TO THE SNOT SQUIRTERS.

YOUR CHOICE.

FINE, BUT AT LEAST TURN OFF THAT DING-BLASTED LIGHT BEFORE MORE BEASTIES FIND US!

NOT YET, I MIGHT NEED THE LIGHT. JUST BUY ME SOME TIME UNTIL I GET US OUT OF THIS.

IT'S WORKING!

oh g-goody... that's the G-G-GOOD N-N-NEWS...

HELP ME CHIP THEM OUT!

THIS IS CRAZY. WE SHOULD BE RUNNIN'!

SHE'S BACK AND I'VE ONLY GOT ABOUT ONE SHOT LEFT!

wanna hear the... B-B-Bad news? ...I'm P-P-P-Passing out...

LUCY'S GOING INTO CHILL-COMA!

YEAH? WELL TURN OFF THAT LIGHT FIRST!

...oh.. ...yeah..

voice...command: Lux-99...omega...

Lights.. ...out...

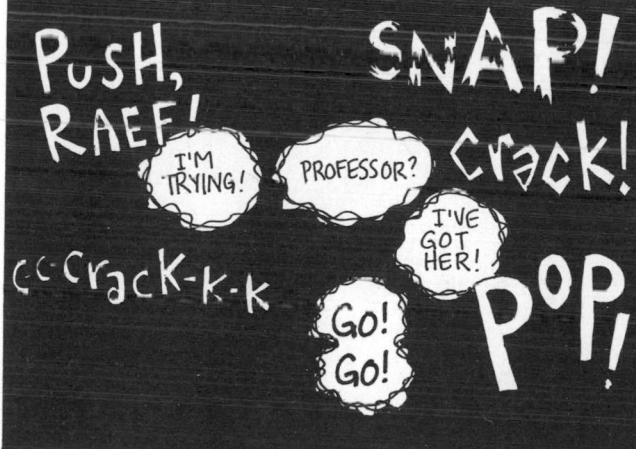

PUSH, RAEF!

SNAP!

I'M TRYING!

PROFESSOR?

crack!

I'VE GOT HER!

c-c-crack-k-k

GO! GO!

POP!

...whoa...

...what...

WHAT HAPPENED?

oh, yeah.

BUT WE MADE IT.

THAT'S GOOD, HUH?

I'M SORRY. I WAS WRONG...

ABOUT THE SCREAMERS AND...uh.

AND A **LOT** OF THINGS.

AFTER ALL OF THE AMAZING STUFF WE'VE SEEN OUT HERE, WHY WOULD YOU DOUBT MA'DOG ABOUT SCREAMERS?

i don't know.

WELL **I** DO. HE GOT ON YOUR NERVES, SO YOU DECIDED TO TAKE CONTROL OF ME AGAINST MY WILL AND ENDANGER US ALL!

OF COURSE, I SHOULD PROBABLY THANK YOU.

BEFORE TONIGHT I USED TO WONDER WHO I WAS, BUT NOW I KNOW:

I'M JUST YOUR FANCY FLASHLIGHT!

WHA—? NO! YOU'RE SO MUCH... I WOULD NEVER TREAT YOU LIKE THAT—

YOU JUST DID, GENIUS.

DO YOU KNOW WHAT THAT FEELS LIKE?

no.

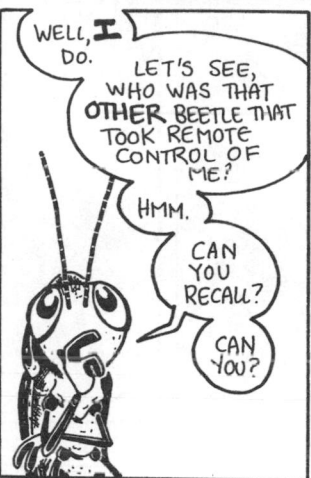

WELL, I DO.

LET'S SEE, WHO WAS THAT OTHER BEETLE THAT TOOK REMOTE CONTROL OF ME?

HMM.

CAN YOU RECALL?

CAN YOU?

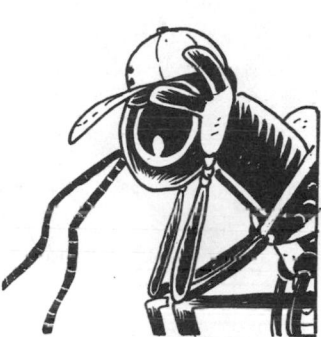

OH, I REMEMBER NOW.

IT WAS THE BAD GUY!

...groan...

SNAP!

ACK, DON'T BE SUCH A WEE, CRYIN' LARVA...

...SHE PROBABLY SAVED YER—

urk!

zziiitp!

AND YOU.

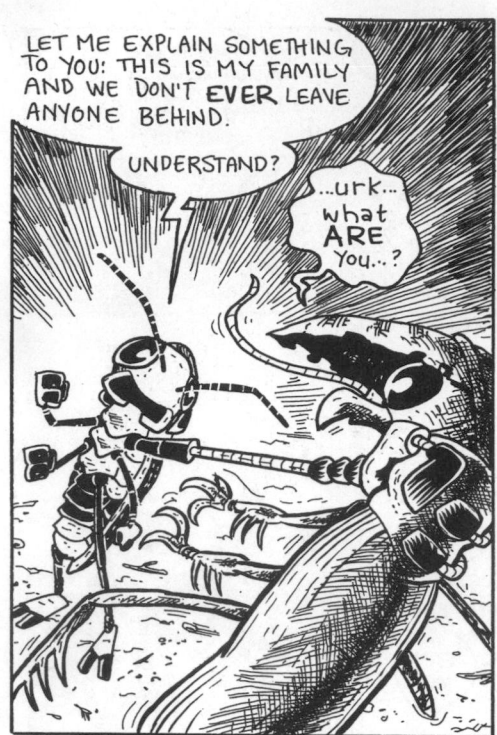

LET ME EXPLAIN SOMETHING TO YOU: THIS IS MY FAMILY AND WE DON'T **EVER** LEAVE ANYONE BEHIND.

UNDERSTAND?

...urk... what **ARE** you...?

I'M **GROUCHY**, THAT'S WHAT I AM!

I'M CONFUSED AND FRUSTRATED.

I DON'T KNOW WHO I AM, AND I'M TRAVELING.

I **HATE** TRAVELING!

RAEF.

RAEF, DEAR, DON'T.

NOT NOW, BEATRICE.

I'M IN NO MOOD FOR—

B-Beatrice?

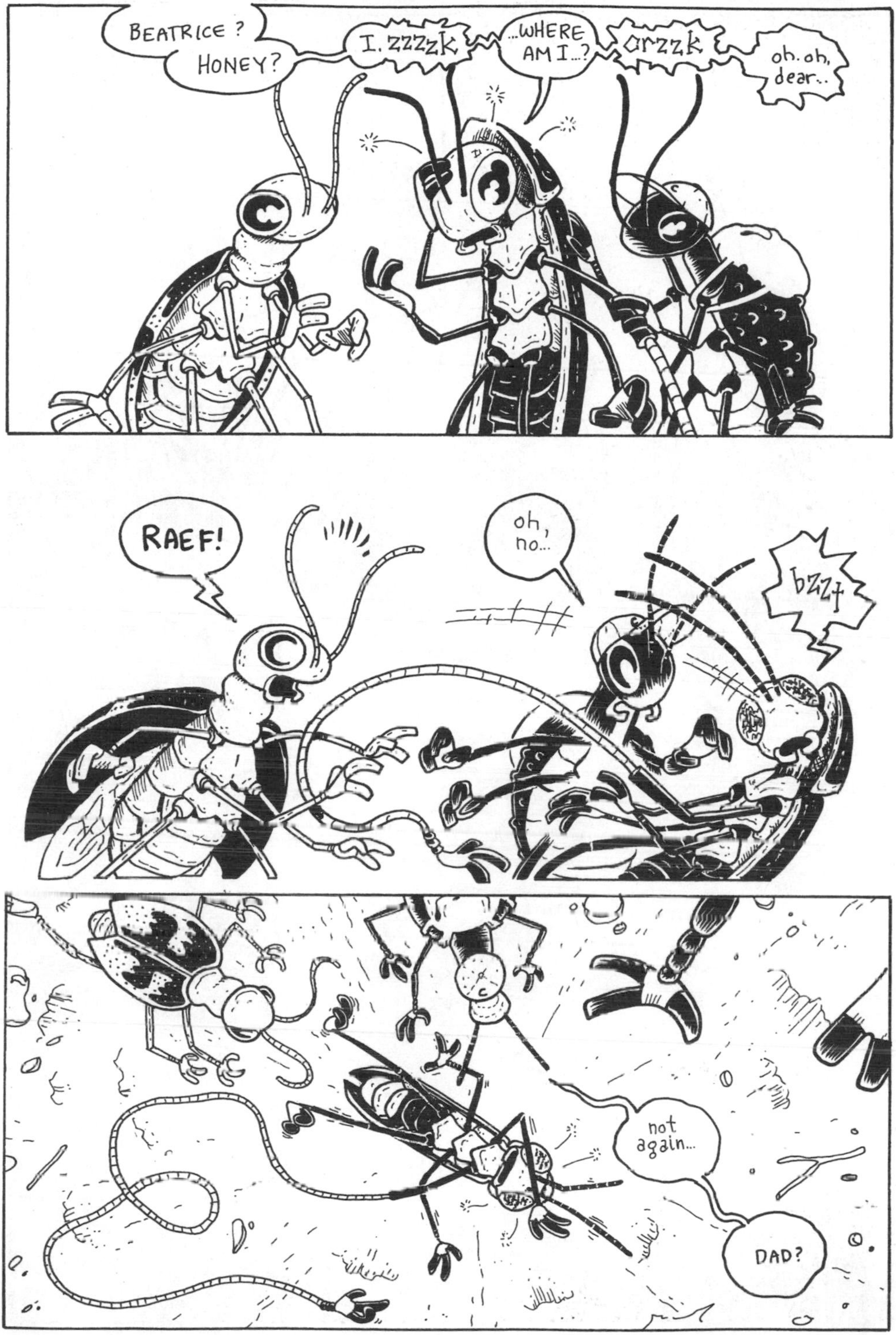

BEATRICE? HONEY?

I. zzzzk

...WHERE AM I...?

orzzk

oh. oh, dear..

RAEF!

oh, no...

bzzt

not again...

DAD?

Chapter 9

BUT...?

I WAS HOPING TO COLLECT A FEW SAMPLES BEFORE I OBLITERATE THEM.

I'M CURIOUS TO KNOW MORE ABOUT THEIR FORMATION.

CURIOUS, MIRIAM?

REALLY?

HAVE YOU FORGOTTEN THE MANTRA OF OUR ORDER?

OF COURSE NOT.

I JUST...

"CURIOSITY LEADS TO QUESTIONS,"

"QUESTIONS LEAD TO DOUBT,"

"AND THERE MUST BE NO DOUBT."

ARTIFACTS LIKE THESE CONTRADICT THE SACRED SCROLLS. THAT CAN LEAD TO DOUBTS ABOUT SCARABUS, BUT THE BEETLES OF COLEOPOLIS MUST **NEVER** DOUBT HIS EXISTENCE. IF THEY DID, THEN THEY WOULD SURELY SPIRAL INTO WICKEDNESS AND DESPAIR.

WE MUST DESTROY THESE STONES TO KEEP OUR PEOPLE SAFE.

BUT.. BUT.. PERHAPS WE COULD LEARN SOMETHING USEFUL FROM THESE STONES.

ABSOLUTELY NOT.

PROCEED WITH THE DEMOLITION.

WITH ALL DUE RESPECT, DR. OWEN, THAT HARDLY SEEMS FAIR.

WHY MUST **I** DESTROY MY DISCOVERY WHEN **YOU** GET TO PARADE ABOUT THAT STONE BEHEMOTH YOU BROUGHT BACK FROM THE DESERT?

SURELY YOU CAN SEE THAT ... **THING** ... IS THE VERY TYPE OF FORBIDDEN KNOWLEDGE THAT WE IN THE ORDER HAVE TRIED TO KEEP HIDDEN FROM THE WORLD?

ARE YOU QUESTIONING MY JUDGEMENT, DR. BEDLOW?

i believe it was a... mistake... to bring it here and reveal it to the public.

IT WAS NO MISTAKE.

HOW CAN YOU BE SO **SURE** OF THAT?

BECAUSE I AM STILL ALIVE.

WHAT DOES **THAT** MEAN?

IF BRINGING THE STONE BEAST FROM THE DESERT WAS A MISTAKE, SCARABUS WOULD HAVE STRUCK ME DOWN BY NOW.

YOU CAN'T BE SERIOUS.

DEADLY SERIOUS.

THAT IS AN ENORMOUS GAMBLE TO TAKE ON SUCH SHAKY LOGIC. DON'T WE RISK PROVOKING SCARABUS INTO DESTROYING **ALL** OF NEW COLEOPOLIS JUST AS HE DESTROYED THE ORIGINAL CITY A THOUSAND YEARS AGO?

OH, MIRIAM, YOU JUST DON'T GET IT.

LET ME TELL YOU A STORY...

LONG BEFORE THE FIRST CATACLYSM, THE ORDER OF THE SCARABI WAS FOUNDED TO DISCOURAGE BEETLES FROM QUESTIONING THE ANCIENT TEXTS. UNFORTUNATELY, THE HERETICS AND DANGEROUS THINKERS WERE TOO POWERFUL AT THAT TIME.

SO, 1000 YEARS AGO, THREE FAITHFUL SCARABI CLIMBED THE GREAT PALM TREE...

...PLANTED EXPLOSIVES AROUND THE THREE COCONUTS...

...AND TRIGGERED THEIR CATACLYSMIC FALL ON COLEOPOLIS.

WHAT?

NO. THOSE COCONUTS FELL BECAUSE IT WAS THE WILL OF SCARABUS.

AND THE THREE SCARABI AGENTS WERE INSTRUMENTS OF THAT WILL. AS AM I. AND AS HIS INSTRUMENT, IT FOLLOWS LOGICALLY THAT ANYTHING I DO MUST BE HIS WILL. THUS, ANYTHING I DO MUST BE CORRECT.

this is madness...

THE ONLY MADNESS WAS THINKING WE COULD STOP DANGEROUS THOUGHTS WITH A FEW COCONUTS.

AND HOW CAN YOU BE SO SURE THAT **GREATER** REVELATIONS MIGHT NOT BE FOUND IN THESE STRANGE FORMS?

AS A FAITHFUL MEMBER OF THE ORDER, IT IS MY DESIRE TO EXCAVATE SOME SAMPLES.

BY YOUR OWN LOGIC, THAT DESIRE **MUST** BE THE WILL OF SCARABUS FOR, AS YOU CAN **SEE**, HE HAS NOT STRUCK ME DOWN.

YET.

YOU MEANT TO SAY, "HE HAS NOT STRUCK ME DOWN **YET**."

ugh.

THESE BUSINESS MEETINGS ARE **SO** EXHAUSTING.

Chapter 10

AFTER RAEF SHUT DOWN, WE CARRIED HIM UNTIL WE FOUND A SAFE PLACE TO HIDE. WE ALSO FOUND WATER. MA'DOG DIDN'T UNDERSTAND WHY WE WERE LOOKING FOR IT IN THE FIRST PLACE.

WAIT... YOU WERE **LOOKING** FOR WATER? LEAVES AND GRASS ARE COVERED IN DEW AT DAWN.

PLUS, YER A **SANDWALKER**. SURELY IF YA CAN PULL WATER FROM THE DESERT AIR, YOU COULD GET IT IN A HUMID FOREST.

RIGHT?

AH HA HA! CITY BEETLES! YA FERGET YER OWN NATURES! TRY TO REMEMBER TO BREATHE WHILE YER WALKING, OKAY?

ONCE WE GOT SETTLED IN A HOLLOWED TREE TRUNK, I REMOVED RAEF'S HEAD FROM HIS BODY. HE HAS A COMPUTER IN HIS THORAX A LOT LIKE THE GANGLION IN OUR THORAX THAT COORDINATES THE MOVEMENT OF OUR LEGS AND WINGS.

SINCE RAEF'S BRAIN REGULATES THE COMPUTER IN HIS THORAX, I FIGURED SEPARATING HIS HEAD AND BODY WOULD GIVE HIS BRAIN LESS TO WORRY ABOUT AND HELP HIM REGAIN CONSCIOUSNESS FASTER. IT'S BEEN A FEW DAYS AND IT SEEMS TO BE WORKING.

SO, IF HE **HATES** BEING TOLD WHAT TO DO, YOU CAN IMAGINE HOW HE FEELS ABOUT BEING REMOTELY CONTROLLED.

THAT SAID, HE DOES REALIZE THAT IF YOU HADN'T TAKEN CONTROL OF HIM AT THAT MOMENT AND TURNED ON HIS LIGHT, YOU WOULD NEVER HAVE SEEN THE SCREAMER COMING.

YOU WOULDN'T HAVE BEEN ABLE TO LEAP OUT OF THE WAY AND, AS A CONSEQUENCE, YOU WOULD BE VERY, **VERY** DEAD RIGHT NOW.

YOUR FATHER MAY NOT REMEMBER WHO HE IS, BUT HE KNOWS HOW HE **FEELS.** BEING CONTROLLED MAY BE UNBEARABLE FOR HIM, BUT LOSING YOU WOULD BE **UNTHINKABLE.**

SO HE **LOVES** ME, HE JUST DOESN'T KNOW **WHY.**

THAT'S ABOUT IT. OF COURSE, THAT'S HOW WE **ALL** FEEL ABOUT YOU.

THANKS, MOM.

WE'LL GET THROUGH THIS.

TOGETHER.

SPEAKING OF WHICH, THERE'S SOMEONE YOU SHOULD SEE BEFORE YOU VISIT YOUR FATHER.

DO I HAFTA?

ABSOLUTELY.

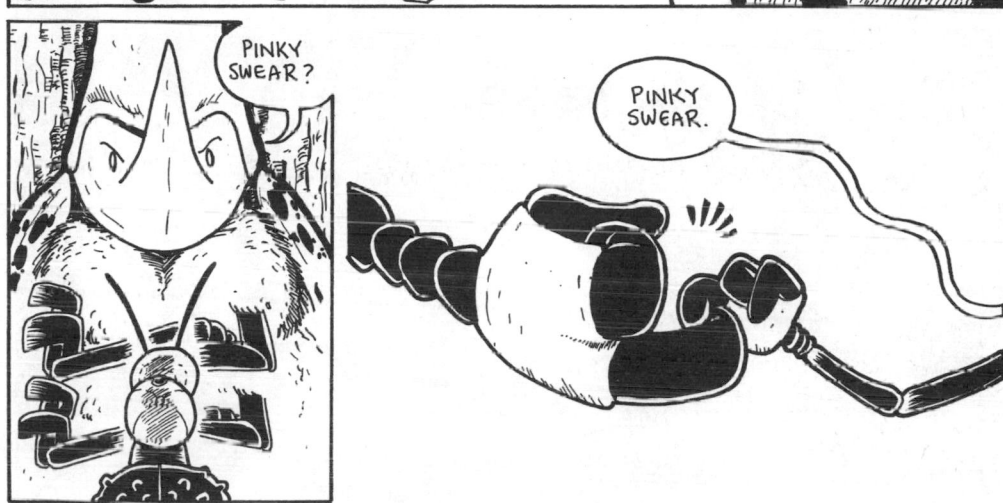

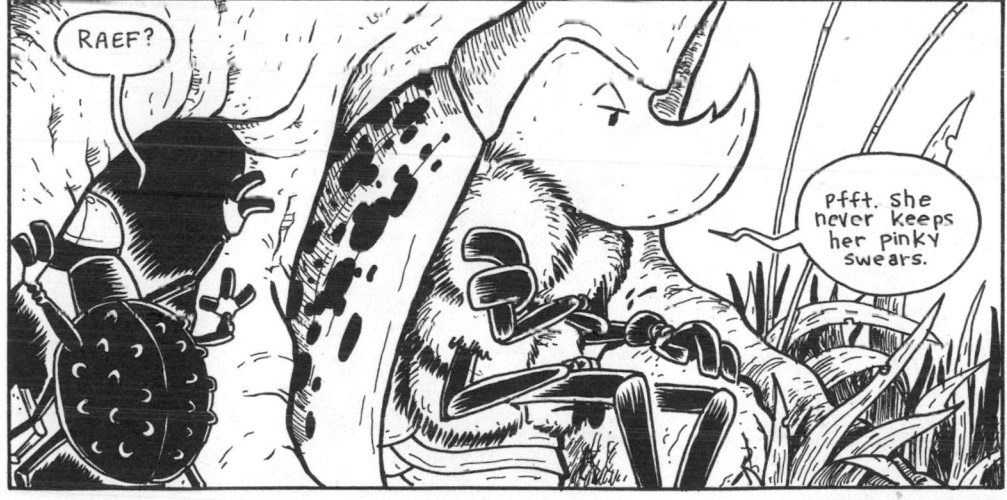

RAEF? MAY I COME IN?

RAEF? ARE YOU OKAY?

PLEASE, SAY SOMETH'

BOO!

AAAH!

HAhaha

...hey.. wait a minute, i forgot...

I'M MAD AT YOU.

..you should be..

I'M SORRY, RAEF.

I KNOW THAT I REALLY MESSED UP.

BUT IF YOU GIVE ME A CHANCE, I THINK I CAN MAKE IT RIGHT.

I'M LISTENING.

THE ONLY REASON I INSTALLED THE REMOTE CONTROL WAS TO PROTECT YOUR LIVING BRAIN. I FIGURED IF YOUR BODY MALFUNCTIONED, I COULD... WELL ... STOP YOU BEFORE YOU HURT YOURSELF.

HOW'S THAT WORKING OUT?

NOT SO GREAT, BUT I HAVE AN IDEA.

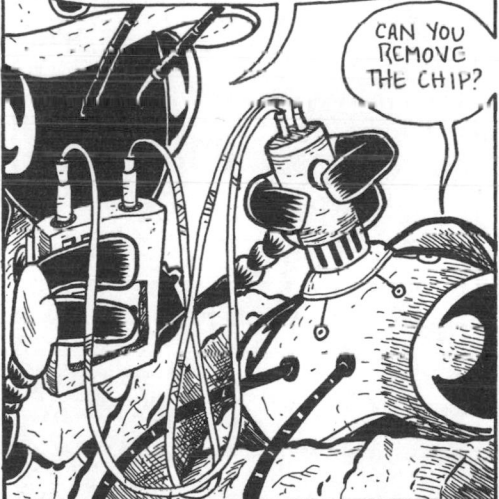

YOUR MEMORY HAS BEEN ON THE VERGE OF RETURNING TWICE NOW, AND BOTH TIMES YOU'VE SHUT DOWN. MAYBE YOUR SUBCONSCIOUS IS REACTING SO VIOLENTLY TO THE REMOTE CONTROL CHIP THAT YOUR ENTIRE SYSTEM DEACTIVATES.

CAN YOU REMOVE THE CHIP?

I THINK SO, BUT YOU'LL NEED TO OPEN YOUR CHEST PLATE.

WIRE ME UP.

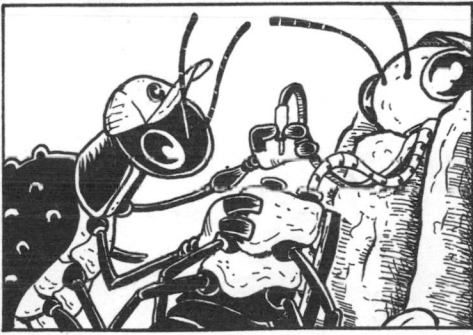

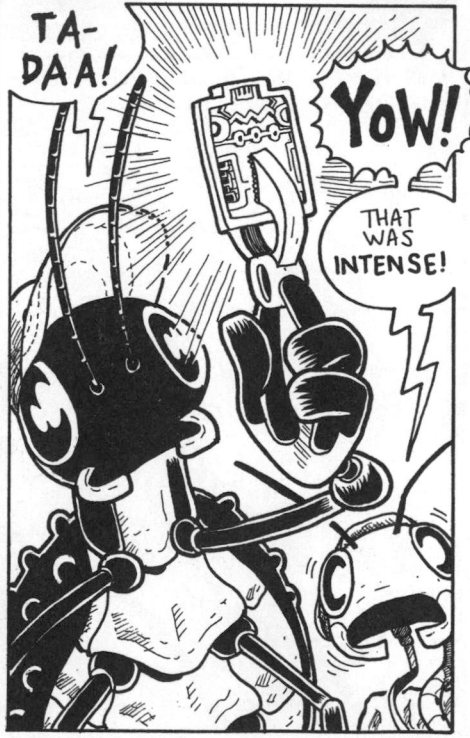

WHEN THE CHIP CAME OUT, IT TRIGGERED A POWERFUL MEMORY.

CAN YOU TELL ME ABOUT IT?

WELL, I'M CRADLING THIS CUTE LITTLE GRUB IN MY ARMS...

...AND, AS I HOLD HER, SHE SAYS...

POPPA, WHEN WE HUG, IT'S LIKE WE'RE...

...completing a love circuit...

OH. HAVE I TOLD YOU THIS STORY BEFORE?

uh...yeah.. ..i guess so...

SORRY. I CAN'T REMEMBER WHAT I'VE SAID OR WHEN I SAID IT. GUESS THINGS ARE MORE JUMBLED IN HERE THAN I THOUGHT.

THEN IT MIGHT TAKE YOU A WHILE TO "ORGANIZE" YOUR THOUGHTS.

HA! GOOD ONE!

IT'S THE KINDA THING MY DAD WOULD SAY.

CLick!

WOW. IT'S A LOT EASIER TO MOVE MY LIMBS ALL OF A SUDDEN.

YEAH, I LUBRICATED YOUR JOINTS WHILE YOU WERE UNCONSCIOUS.

"OIL" BE EXCITED TO TRY THEM OUT.

I SAID "OIL," INSTEAD OF "I'LL."

I GET IT. THAT WAS JUST STUNNED SILENCE.

WHAT? THAT WAS A GOOD ONE.

THE MERE FACT THAT YOU THINK THAT TELLS ME YOU NEED MORE REST.

WAIT. I NEED TO DO SOMETHING BEFORE YOU DISCONNECT ME.

I TOOK A PICTURE OF THE SCREAMER WITH THAT FANCY CAMERA THAT TAKES PICTURES OF CRITTERS' INSIDES.

LOOK. YOU CAN SEE ITS BUNS.

BZZZZ

BONES.

RIGHT.

THANKS, PAGE. THIS IS GREAT.

HAP-P-P-P- ZZZK... HAPPY TO DO IT—ZZZK... PERFESSOR.

OKAY, TIME TO REST THAT BRAIN.

I'LL CHECK ON YOU IN A BIT.

I'LL BE HERE.

MOSSY?

...AND THEN THE LITTLE ANT APPROACHED THE MIGHTY GRASSHOPPER...

WHAT'S GOING ON?

MA'DOG IS ENTERTAINING THE WHIRLIGIG BEETLES.

THE, WHO, NOW?

US!

US! US! US! US!

THESE REMARKABLE BEETLES LIVE ON THE SURFACE OF THE WATER.

OUR EYES ARE SPLIT.

THE TOP TWO FOR LOOKING IN THE AIR.

THE BOTTOM TWO FOR LOOKING AT YOUR UNDERWEAR!

HEE HEE! SHE MEANS UNDER-**WATER.**

Y'KNOW, JUST BETWEEN YOU AND ME? I THINK HE NEEDS A LITTLE MORE QUIET TIME.

mmmm.

HAVE YOU SEEN MOSSY?

HE SAID HE WAS GOING FOR A WALK ALONG THE BANK.

FOLLOW MEEE ELIZA SAID TO HIM I'LL TAKE YOU WHERE THE RIVER KISSES YOUR SKIN

?

ELIZA, I WOULD LIKE TO FOLLOW YOU...

BUT MY MA AND PA, THEY WOULD NOT WANT ME TO

BLOOP!

footer 195

RAEF! RAEF, ANSWER ME!

please be okay.

please be okay.

this CANNOT be happening...

ELSEWHERE...

uh... hello?

I WAS JUST DOZING A BIT AND... uh...

COULD YOU TELL ME WHERE WE'RE GOING?

I MEAN, I'VE HEARD OF LETTING YOUR MIND WANDER, BUT THIS IS RIDICULOUS.

GET IT?

I'VE SORTA LOST MY HEAD.

HEH.

ANYBODY?

Chapter 11

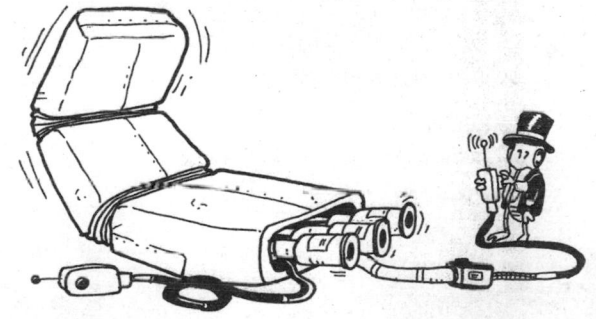

201

SO WHICH PART IS IN THE WATER?

BEATS ME.

BOOP BEEP

BOOP

ACTIVATE THE REMOTE CONTROL TO GET THE BODY TO RETURN.

I... I CAN'T.

I KNOW YOU PROMISED NOT TO USE THE REMOTE CONTROL AGAIN, BUT THIS IS AN EMERGENCY!

NO, I REALLY CAN'T.

i removed the remote control chip.

ARE YOU SERIOUS? YOU PINKY SWORE NOT TO DO ANYTHING STUPID!

I THOUGHT I WAS DOING THE RIGHT THING.

THE RIGHT THING AT THE WRONG TIME!

HOW WAS I SUPPOSED TO KNOW THAT?

STOP IT!

DO YOU HAVE ANOTHER DETECTOR?

YES, IN MY—

Boop BEEP BOOP

Beep Boop Boop

GIVE ME THIS ONE.

O-OKAY.

ONE PART OF YOUR FATHER IS UNDERWATER AND THE OTHER IS HEADING INTO THE FOREST. WE DON'T KNOW WHICH IS THE BRAIN, SO WE NEED TO ACT **FAST**.

MA'DOG AND I ARE GOING TO FOLLOW THE SIGNAL IN THE WOODS AND YOU TWO ARE GOING TO RETRIEVE THE BIT IN THE POND.

uh... MAYBE WE SHOULDN'T SPLIT UP...

Yer hat, Ma'am.

Thank you.

TIME IS SHORT, LUCY.

WE CAN TAKE CARE OF OURSELVES.

AYE.

BUT HOW ARE WE SUPPOSED TO—?

BE CLEVER, DEAR.

QUICKLY.

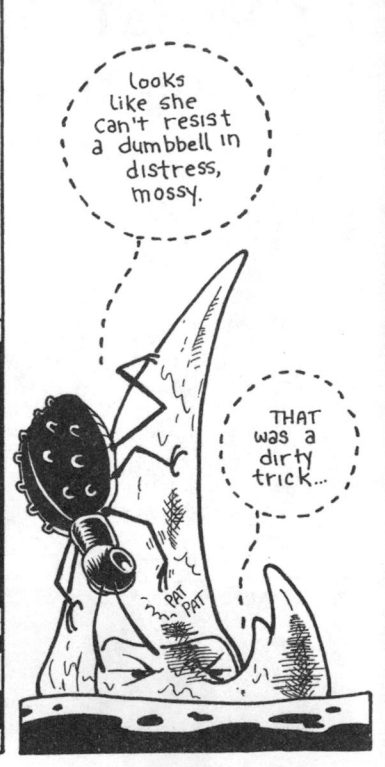

I ONLY CALLED YOU THAT BECAUSE YOU CALLED ME "GENIUS."

YOU **KNOW** I HATE THAT.

YEAH, YEAH.

I LEFT MY POST AND NOW DAD'S GONE.

THIS IS MY FAULT AND I'M GONNA FIX IT.

BUT **SHE** CAN DO IT.

WE'LL GIVE HER THE DETECTOR.

PLUS, YOU ALMOST DROWNED.

TWICE.

SHOULDN'T YOU BE WORKING ON SOME BRILLIANT INVENTION TO MAKE MY LITTLE UNDERWATER ADVENTURE POSSIBLE?

…

IF A BUBBLE OF AIR COULD BE TRAPPED UNDER THE ELYTRA, IT **MIGHT** BE POSSIBLE TO USE IT TO BREATHE.

IN AN IDEAL SITUATION, AS YOU BREATHE OXYGEN INTO YOUR TRACHEAE, MORE OXYGEN WOULD DIFFUSE IN FROM THE WATER TO REPLENISH THE BUBBLE.

IN THEORY, A BEETLE DOING THIS COULD STAY UNDERWATER LONGER THAN THE INITIAL SUPPLY OF OXYGEN IN THE BUBBLE WOULD PREDICT.

ELYTRA

AIR BUBBLE (UNDER ELYTRA)

TRACHEAE (BREATHING HOLES)

IN THEORY?

THE GAS LAWS SAY IT WILL WORK.

IT WORKS, ALL RIGHT.

THAT'S HOW **I** STAY UNDER.

A MONSTER RISES!
DEATH FROM BELOW!
SWIM FOR YOUR LIVES!
YEESH. WHAT'S UP WITH THE WHIRLIGIGS?
WE'RE NOT GONNA STICK AROUND TO FIND OUT!
LET'S GO!
oh, my...
Bubble
Bubble
Bubble
Bubble
Bubble
BEEP
BOOP
BOOP
BEEP
BEEP
HOLY MOLEY! THE DETECTOR IS GOING NUTS!

BOOP
BEEP
BOOP
BEEP
BOOP
BEEP
BOOP
BEEP
BOOP
BEEP
BOOP
BEEP
BOOP
BEEP
BOOP
BEEP
BOOP
BEEP
BOOP
BEEP
BOOP
BEEP
BOOP
BEEP
BOOP
BEEP

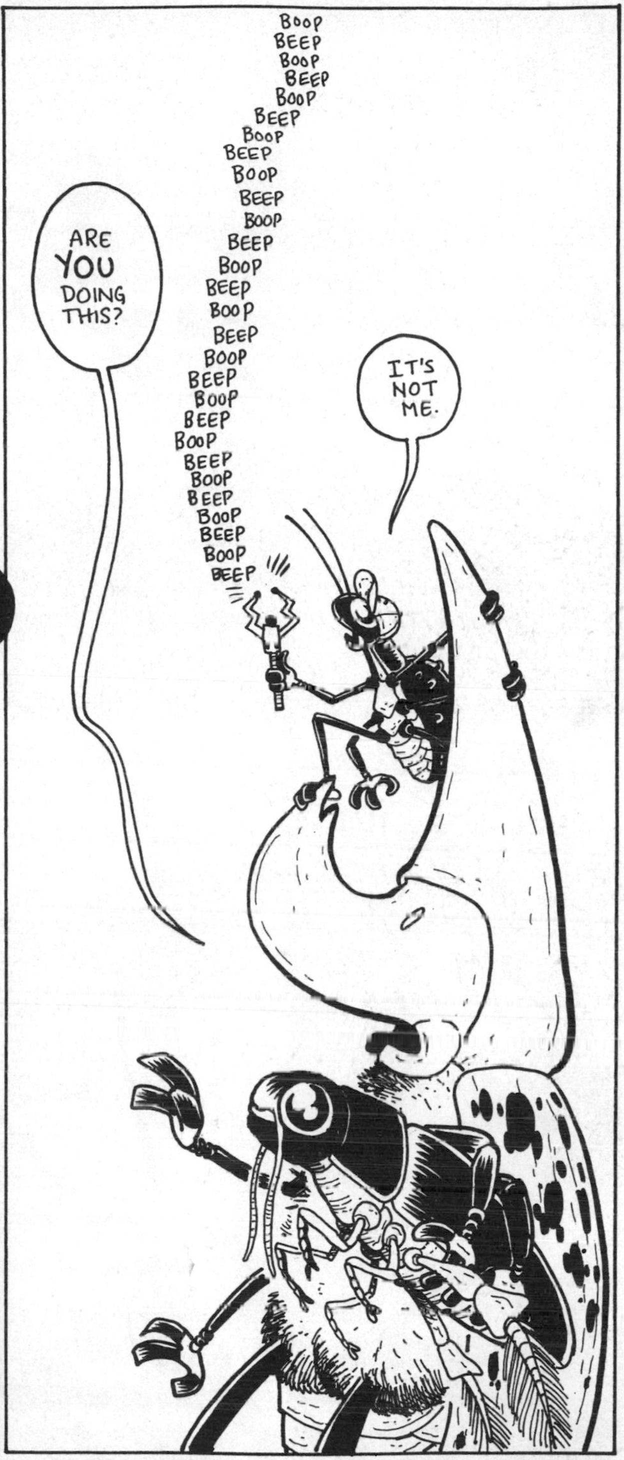

ARE YOU DOING THIS?

IT'S NOT ME.

POP

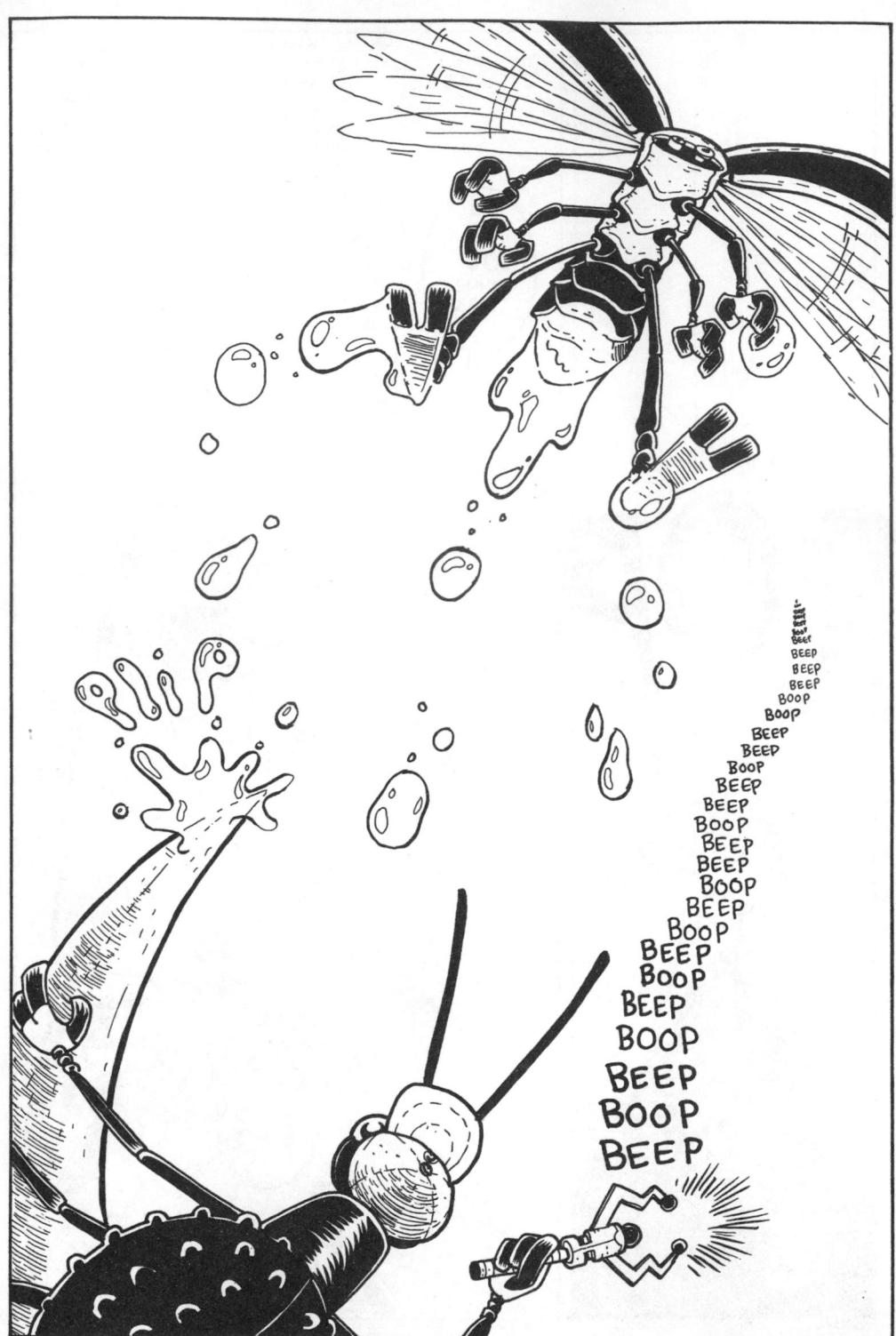

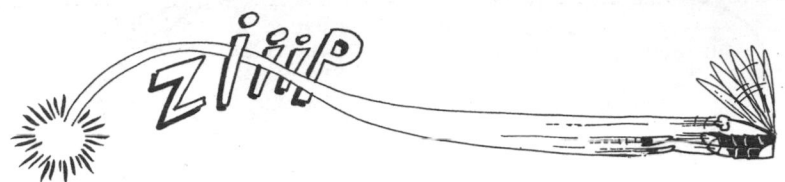

Chapter 12

AND THAT IS WHAT WILL HAPPEN TO YOU AND ME IF WE DON'T MAKE THIS LITTLE **FRAUD** HELP US.

WE CAN'T JUST GO AROUND GRABBING OTHER BEETLES AND ENSLAVING THEM. IT ISN'T RIGHT.

I COULDN'T AGREE MORE. THIS IS SUPER-DUPER WRONG.

BEEP BEEP

WE'VE NO OTHER CHOICE. YER LITTLE DOOHICKEY SAYS THAT A PIECE OF YER MATE IS IN THAT ANT COLONY. NOW, WE CAN'T ASK NICE AND WE CAN'T JUST REACH IN THERE AND GRAB IT. WE NEED TO INFILTRATE THE NEST.

BUT... HE'S SO SMALL.

HEY!

DON'T LET HIS SIZE FOOL YA. THIS ONE IS A CONNIVING, DUPLICITOUS **MONSTER.**

YOOUU WAAANT TO LEEET ME GOOOOOOO

WHY IS HE WIGGLING HIS ABDOMEN LIKE THAT?

HE'S TRYIN' TA TOUCH ME WITH HIS APPEASEMENT GLAND.

IT WON'T WORK ON US, YOU FREELOADER.

LET ME GOOOOOOO

IT RELEASES A CHEMICAL THAT CALMS THE ANTS.

PUTS THE SUPPRESSION ON THEIR AGGRESSION, SO'S THEY DON'T GOBBLE ME UP.

YOU SPEAK THE SAME CHEMICAL LANGUAGE?

YEP. WE ROVE BEETLES KNOW THEIR PHEROMONE CODE.

WHAT'S IT DOING?

YOUR FATHER'S HEAD IS IN THAT ANT COLONY. IT LOOKS LIKE HIS BODY IS... TRYING TO REACH IN AND GRAB IT.

HMPH. HE BETTER HURRY. IT WON'T BE LONG BEFORE A BAZILLION ANTS ARE SWARMING ALL OVER HIM.

THEN WE NEED TO BUY HIM SOME TIME.

LET'S GO!

WHOA.

YOU'RE NOT GOING ANYWHERE.

WHA-?

WE'VE GOTTA SAVE HIM.

NO. WE'VE GOTTA SAVE HIM.

YOU STAY PUT.

BUT I—

—CAN'T FLY TO SAFETY LIKE WE CAN.

BUT, I...

...DON'T SPRAY TOXIC CHEMICALS.

BUT, I...

...DON'T HAVE BIG, NASTY, ANT-CHEWIN' MANDIBLES.

...but...

SIT ON THIS WEE BEETLE AND STAY OUT OF HARM'S WAY.

but...

SIT. ON. HIM.

SO? WHAT'S YOUR STORY?

GAH!

KEEP THEM OFF OF RAEF'S ARMS.

THIS IS GONNA BE SOME REAL WORK, CITY SLICKERS.

ANT COLONIES ARE FULL OF TWISTY-TURNY TUNNELS.

HE COULD BE POKIN' AROUND FOR HOURS.

POP POP

POP POP

GET — OFF — OF

..ewww...

POP!

KEEP GOING.

DON'T SLOW DOWN.

CAN'T HELP IT. I'M GETTIN' FULL.

POP!

GAH. I HATE THESE THINGS!

oh, dear.

I'M RUNNING OUT OF JUICE!

HURRY UP, YOU DING-BLASTED METAL MORON!

Pfsss

THERE ARE TOO MANY OF THEM.

WE NEED A NEW PLAN FAST!

WAY AHEAD OF YOU, BIG BROTHER.

HEY.

HOWDY.

MY, MY, AREN'T YOU A CLEVER BEETLE?

WHAT? THIS LITTLE TRICK?

NAH.

I HAD LOTSA TIME TO FIGURE OUT THE BROADCAST SUBROUTINES LUCY INSTALLED IN MY SOFTWARE AND WRITE A HOMING PROGRAM WHICH I COULD SEND TO THE COMPUTER PROCESSOR IN MY BODY. ONCE I GOT THE BODY HERE, IT WAS EASY ENOUGH FOR MY TELESCOPING ARMS TO FIND MY NOGGIN.

STILL PRETTY IMPRESSIVE.

YEAH, WELL I DID A LOT OF THINKING IN THERE.

I JUST FIGURED IT WAS TIME...

...TO PULL MYSELF TOGETHER.

CLick

giggle

SO, WHAT HAPPENED?

NOT SURE.

THESE ANT THINGS APPEAR TO BE FORAGERS. THEY CARRIED MY HEAD TO THEIR NEST AND STORED ME WITH A BUNCH OF SEEDS THAT SMELLED A LOT LIKE THE OIL YOU USED TO LUBRICATE MY PARTS.

I DIN'T AST TA BE ADOPTED.

IT'S NO PROBLEM, REALLY.

SO BE IT.

WHAT'S THE PLAN?

BEATS ME.

ASK OUR FEARLESS LEADER.

SHOOT, I DON'T EVEN KNOW HOW FAR WE ARE FROM HOME.

I DO.

WHAT?

WOULD YOU CARE TO SHARE WITH THE GROUP?

SURE. WHILE I WAS IN THE ANT COLONY, I FIGURED OUT HOW TO USE OUR RELATIVE POSITION IN THE EARTH'S MAGNETIC FIELD TO CALCULATE OUR DISTANCE FROM THE OASIS.

AND?

THEN I CALCULATED HOW LONG IT WOULD TAKE US TO GET HOME AT OUR CURRENT SPEED.

YES?

YES?

IT'LL BE ABOUT TWENTY YEARS.

20?

years?

IS 100 KILOMETERS PER HOUR FAST ENOUGH?

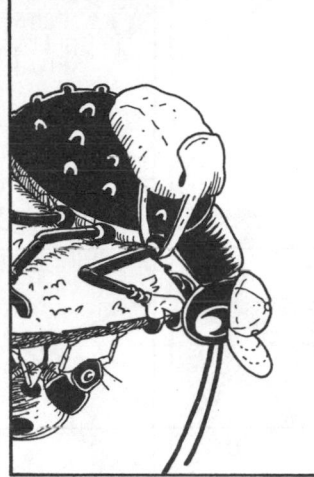

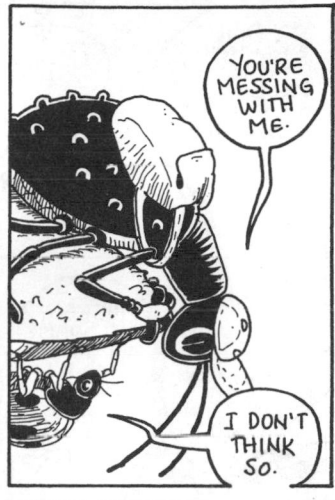

YOU'RE MESSING WITH ME.

I DON'T THINK SO.

HOW CAN A LITTLE BEETLE LIKE YOU GO THAT FAST?

WHEN WE MIGRATE, LADYBUGS RIDE WIND RIVERS **HIGH** IN THE SKY.

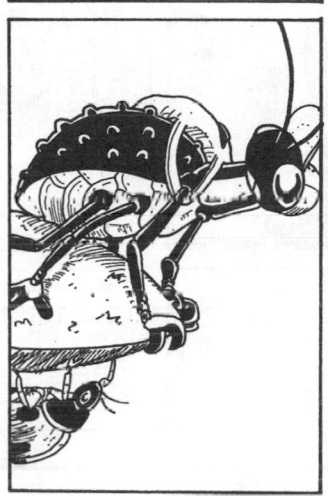

YOU **ARE** MESSING WITH ME.

NO, MA'AM

HOW HIGH ARE THESE CURRENTS?

SUPER-DUPER HIGH. 3000... 5000 FEET.

GREAT.

WE'RE BACK TO DOOMED AGAIN.

WE MIGHT BE ABLE TO USE THIS, DEAR.

Chapter 13

AND LOSERS CERTAINLY DON'T UPEND NUMEROUS SCIENTIFIC ASSUMPTIONS ABOUT NATURE.

MAYBE I SHOULD WRITE THAT IN MY JOURNAL FOR ALL OF POSTERITY TO REMEMBER.

WHAT'S THAT?

JUST A SKETCH. I WAS TRYING TO IMAGINE WHAT THE DESERT GIANT LOOKED LIKE WITH FLESH ON HER BONES.

PAW? TARSUS?

CLAW? not seen in desert.

ears? Like mouse?

MUSCLES??

KINDA LOOKS LIKE A HUE-MON.

A WHAT?

A HUE-MON. SHORT FOR HUE MONKEY. THEY'RE MOSTLY HAIRLESS APES.

BIG.

LOUD

CLEVER, I SUPPOSE.

WHY HUE? ARE THEY BRIGHTLY COLORED?

OH, NO. WE CALL THEM THAT AS A JOKE.

THEY'RE JUST VARYING SHADES OF BROWN.

THEY ACTUALLY PAINT THEMSELVES TO APPEAR MORE INTERESTING.

DO THEY LIVE AROUND HERE?

HAVEN'T SEEN ANY RECENTLY, BUT THEY'RE PESTS. THEY POP UP EVERYWHERE.

REALLY? I GOTTA SEE—

LUCY.

IT'S TIME TO GO, DEAR.

BUT

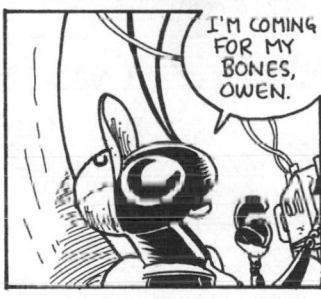
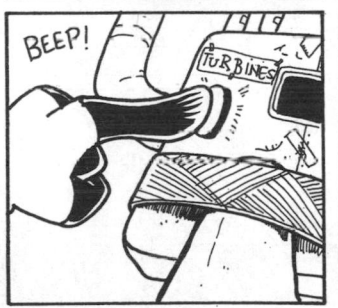

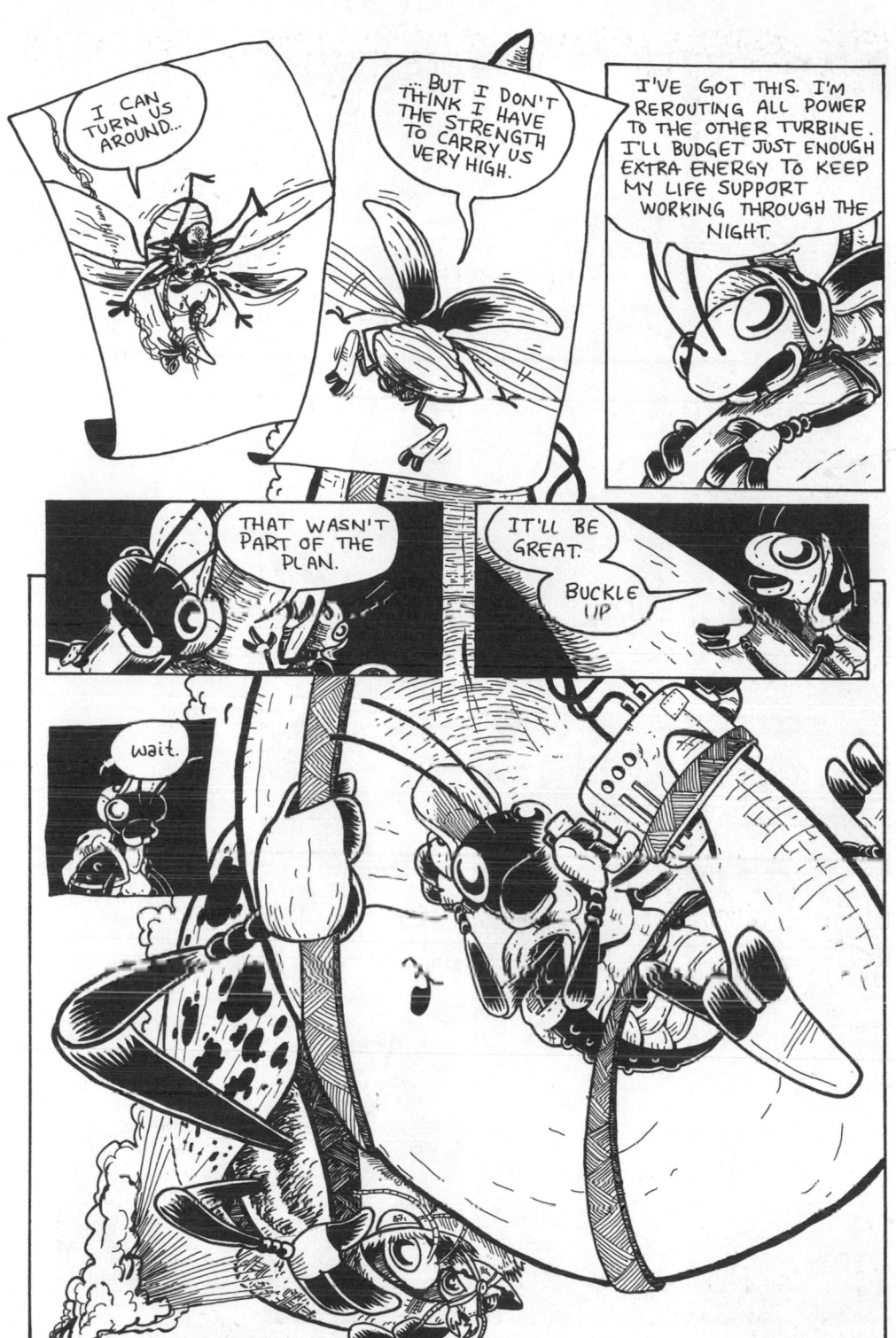

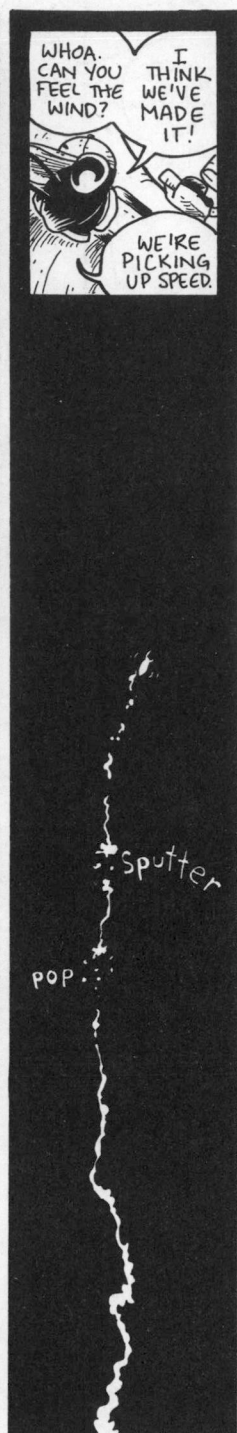

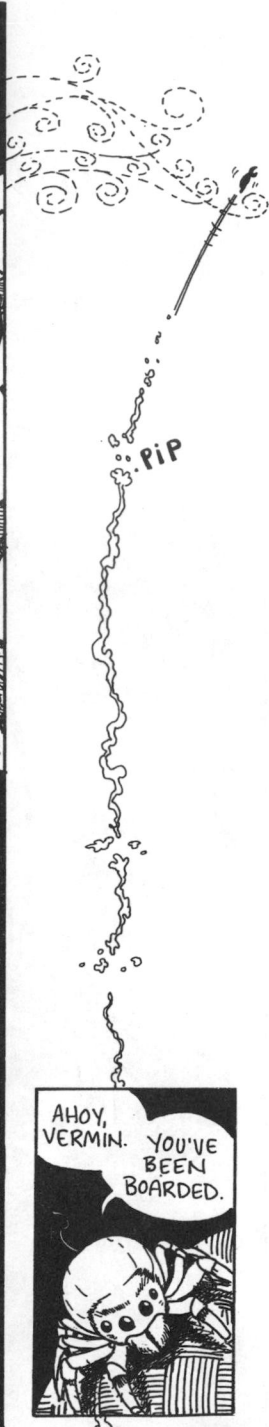

250

SPIDERS? IN THE SKY?

YOU FLEW INTO OUR SILK FILAMENTS, FOOL.

I DIDN'T SEE A WEB.

THERE WASN'T ONE, CRETIN.

WE DISPERSE BY RIDING ON A LITTLE STRAND OF SILK THAT CATCHES THE WIND.

THEY CALL IT "BALLOONING."

BUT YOU CAN CALL IT YOUR DOOOOOOM!

GET RID OF THEM.

NOW.

AYE, AYE.

WHAT? NO. YOU MUST SUBMiiiiiiiiiiT...

CAN I EAT THIS ONE?

NO EXTRA WEIGHT!

LUCKY.

THAT WAS WEIRD.

UH,

ANTS, TOO?

WE APPEAR TO BE SHARING THIS CURRENT WITH A VARIETY OF INSECTS, DEAR.

ANY SIGN OF SCREAMERS?

NO.

OUR COURSE HAS SHIFTED. BEAR LEFT, MOSSY.

GOT IT.

IT'S COLD UP HERE.

I'M GETTING KINDA SLEEPY..

GUYS?

ZZZZZZZ

GREAT. I HADN'T THOUGHT ABOUT CHILL-COMA.

GUESS I'M NEXT.

YEP, AND THE BIGGEST COOLS DOWN THE SLOWEST.

PUT THE NAVIGATION COMPASS WHERE I CAN SEE IT.

I'LL KEEP US ON COURSE FOR AS LONG AS I CAN.

Y'KNOW, MOSSY, IF THESE AIR CURRENTS DON'T GET US HOME ... IF SOMETHING GOES WRONG, I JUST WANT YOU TO KNOW THAT—

IS THIS ABOUT MY ANTENNAE?

AGAIN?

YOU LOST THEM BECAUSE OF ME.

Ugh. WE'VE BEEN OVER THIS A ZILLION TIMES.

IT'S ANCIENT HISTORY.

IT WASN'T YOUR FAULT WE WERE JUMPED BY A GANG OF HOODED GOONS.

BUT I RAN.

RUN!

BECAUSE I **TOLD** YOU TO RUN.

WE ALL KNOW OWEN SENT THEM. IF YOU HAD STAYED THEY PROBABLY WOULD HAVE DRAGGED YOU OUT OF TOWN AND PULLED YOU APART FOR BEING DIFFERENT.

AND INSTEAD, THEY GOT **YOU** AND PULLED OUT YOUR ANTENNAE SO YOU WOULDN'T HAVE TO ENDURE MY "UNHOLY" STINK ANYMORE.

AND FOR THAT I'VE ALWAYS BEEN GRATEFUL.

YOU JOKE BUT I JUST... I WISH I COULD **FIX** IT SOMEHOW.

ZEET ZEET ZEET

ZEET ZEET ZEET

ZEET ZEET

PROFESSOR?

PROFESSOR? ARE YOU IN THERE?

WHAT IS IT?

LAB 41 PRIVATE

ZEET ZEET ZEET ZEET ZEET ZEET

THE DETECTOR YOU TOLD ME TO MONITOR IS BEEPING AND BLINKING LIKE CRAZY.

ZEET ZEET

WHAT DOES IT MEAN, SIR?

IT MEANS, CAPTAIN...

...I'LL BE TESTING THIS SOONER THAN I EXPECTED.

THE NEXT MORNING

ugh.

everybody okay?

AYE.

RAEF IS CHARGING.

ANYONE WANT A DRINK? MY ELYTRA ARE SOAKED WITH FOG.

WHERE ARE WE?

FAMILIAR TERRITORY.

LOOKS LIKE WE STAYED ON COURSE DESPITE THE CHILL-COMA.

no way..

THE STANDING STONE, DEAR. I BELIEVE YOU SAID IT "POINTS THE WAY."

AND, IF I RECALL CORRECTLY, I SAID IT LOOKED LIKE A TOMBSTONE...

Chapter 14

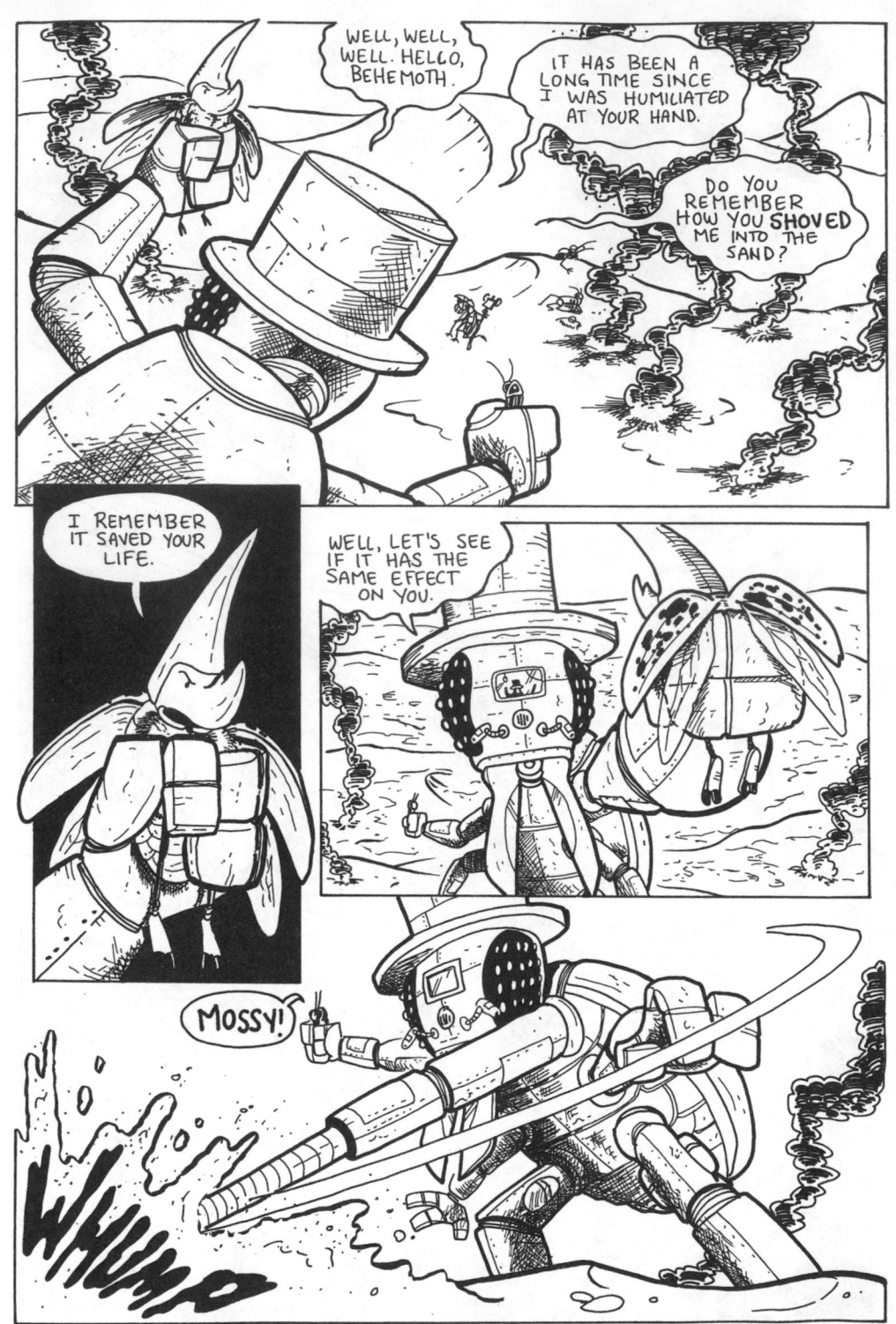

GIT OFFA HIM!

BINK

GRAB!

WHAT HAVE WE HERE?

LEGGO!

CAN IT BE?

A KAMA-SHEEBAY?

I THOUGHT WE ENDED YOUR POISONOUS STORIES AGES AGO.

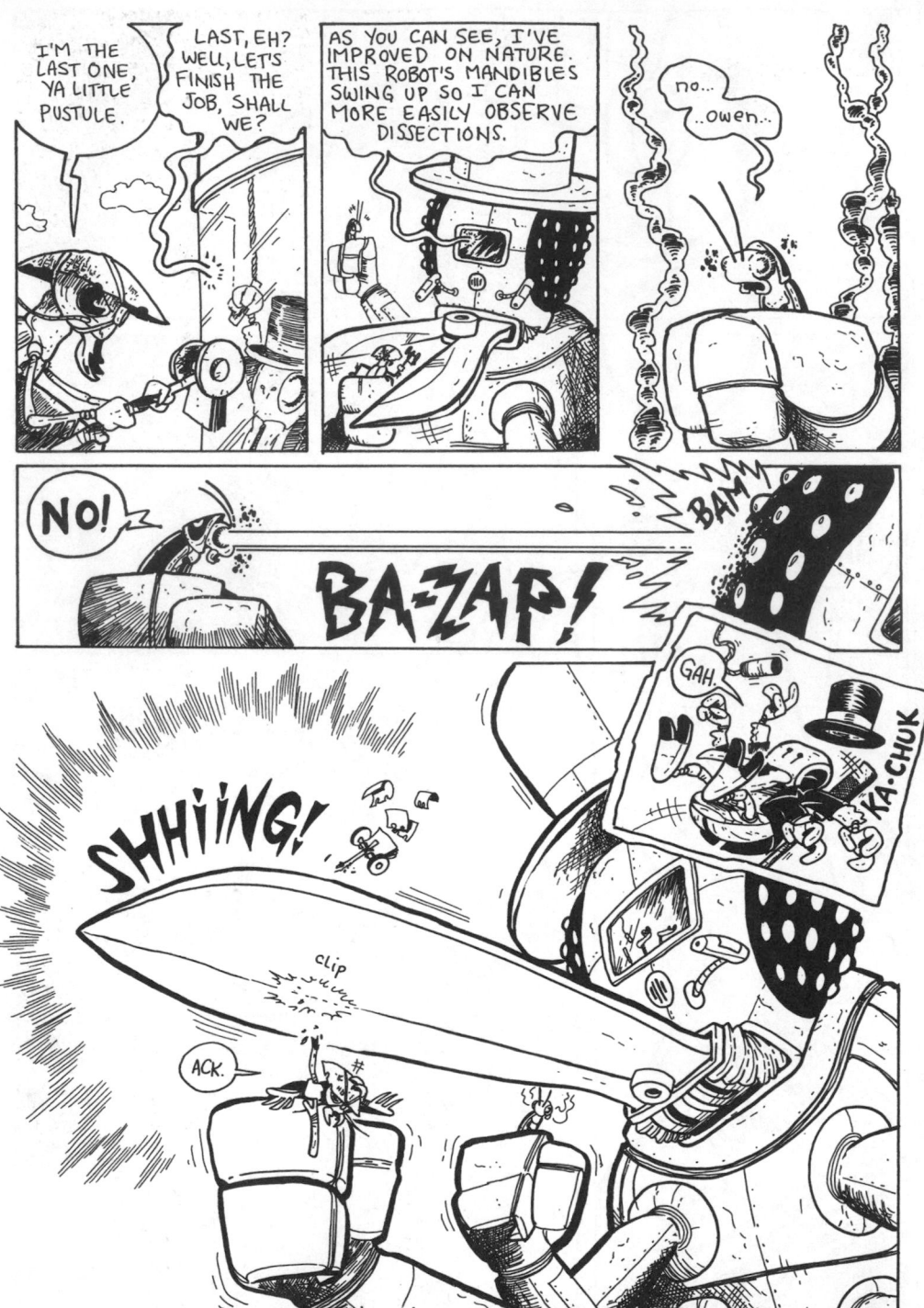

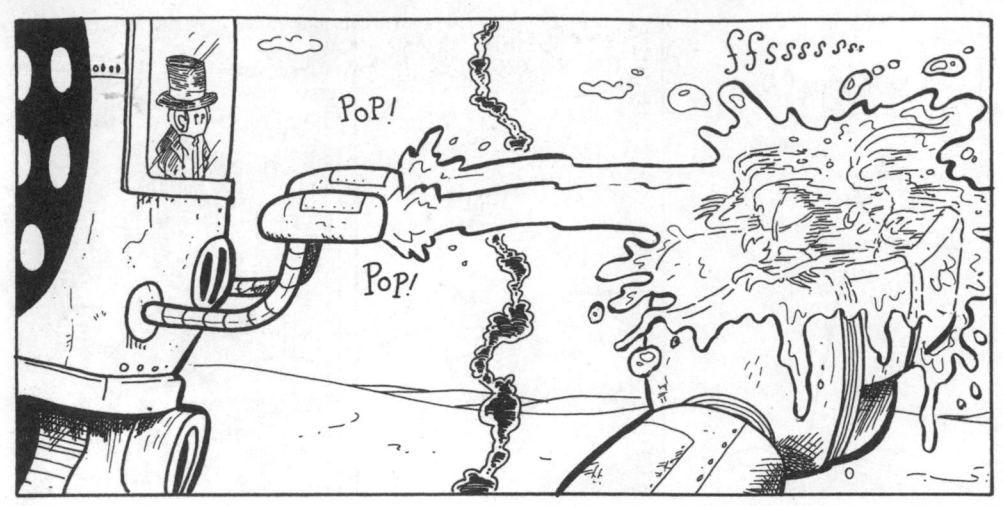

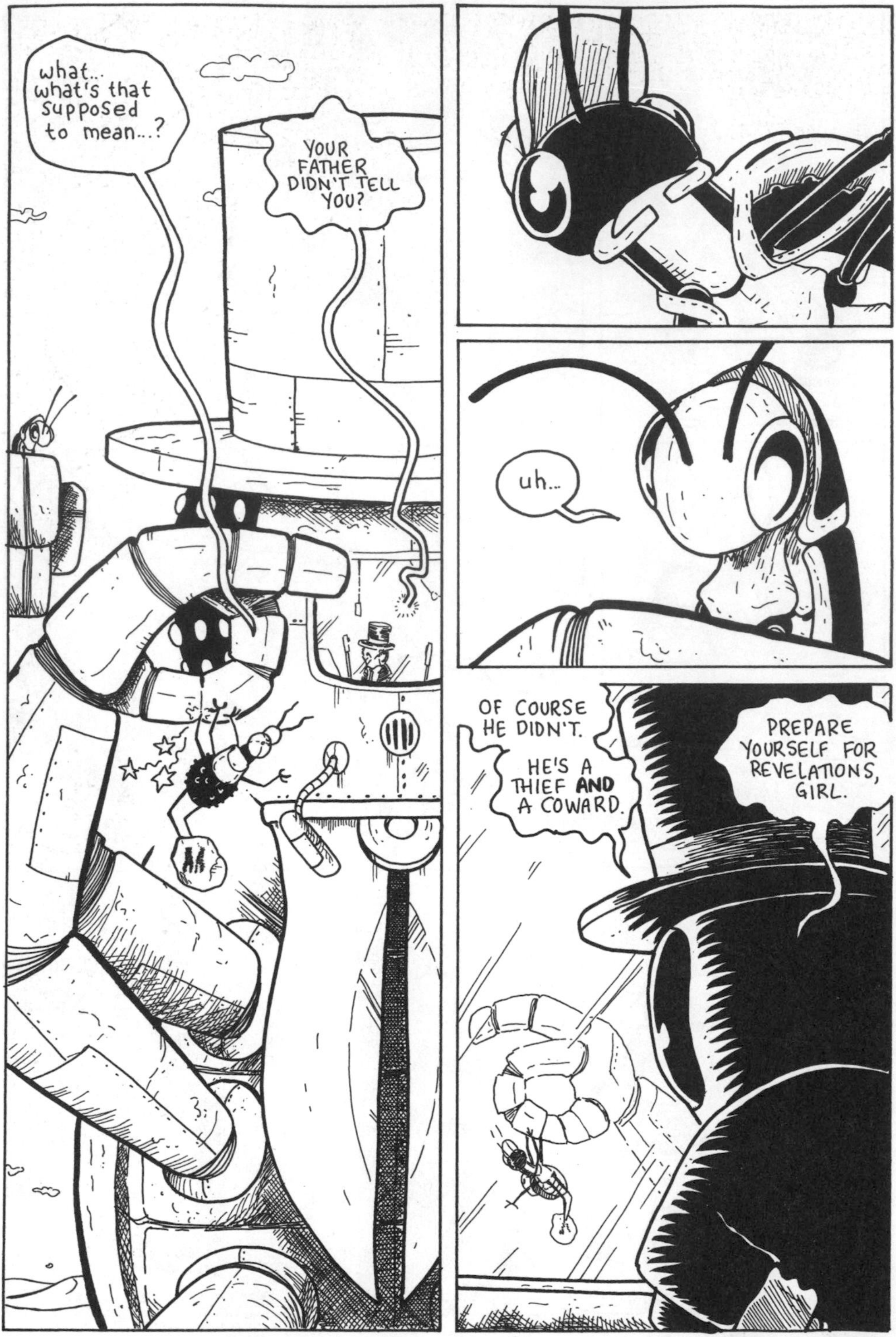

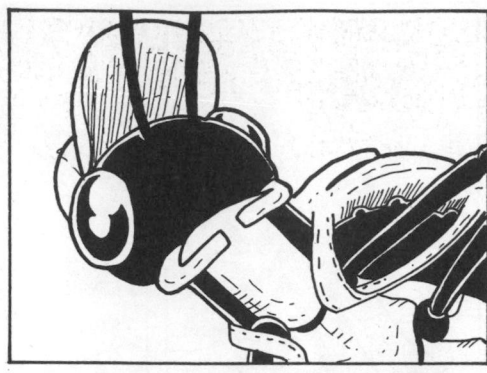

OVER A CENTURY AGO, MY ANCESTORS HELPED EXPUNGE SANDWALKERS LIKE YOU FROM THE OASIS. IT WAS A SPECTACULAR SUCCESS. WITHOUT THEM, WE NO LONGER TRAVELED THE DESERT. THE BEETLES OF NEW COLEOPOLIS BECAME ISOLATED FROM THE INIQUITIES OF THE WORLD.

AS A TROPHY, MY ANCESTORS KEPT THE LAST SANDWALKER EGG SUSPENDED FOREVER IN A CRYPTOBIOTIC CHAMBER.

check it out, Raef.

IT WAS OUR MOST PRIZED HEIRLOOM. SEALED IN A HIDDEN VAULT, IT WAS A SIGN OF OUR ETERNAL POWER.

BUT WHEN I WAS A GRUB, I MADE THE FOOLISH MISTAKE OF SHOWING IT TO MY "BEST" FRIEND.

A FEW YEARS LATER, THE EGG DISAPPEARED. A FEW MONTHS AFTER **THAT**, YOU COMPLETED METAMORPHOSIS AND I KNEW THE TRUTH.

MY FORMER FRIEND AND HIS MISFIT FAMILY HAD STOLEN YOU.

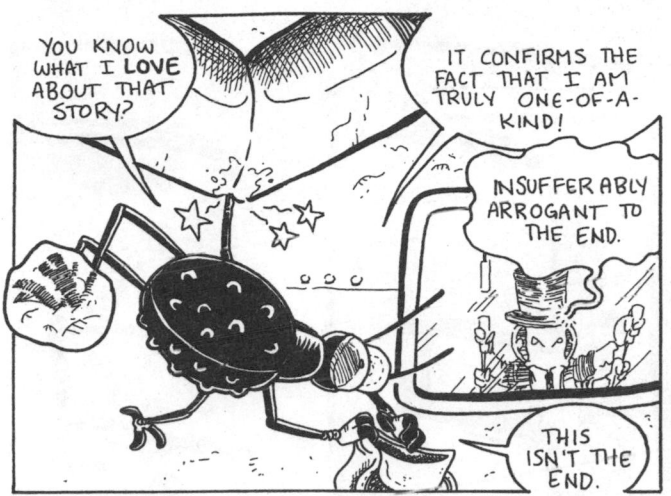

YOU KNOW WHAT I **LOVE** ABOUT THAT STORY?

IT CONFIRMS THE FACT THAT I AM TRULY ONE-OF-A-KIND!

INSUFFERABLY ARROGANT TO THE END.

THIS ISN'T THE END.

OF COURSE IT IS. I HAVE DISPATCHED EVERYONE IN YOUR FAMILY. EVEN YOUR LUMBERING BROTHER CAN'T SAVE YOU THIS TIME.

HE ALREADY HAS.

HE SHOWED ME THAT YOU HAVE TO BE WILLING TO MAKE SACRIFICES FOR YOUR FAMILY.

THAT KNIFE CAN'T CUT THROUGH MY METAL FINGERS.

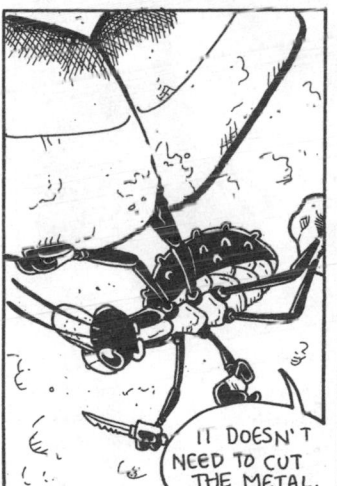

IT DOESN'T NEED TO CUT THE METAL.

LUCY? NO... ...your hand...

it's a good trade, pop.

LUCY!

DELIGHTFUL.

EEEEEEEEEEEE

BRAVO! BRAVO!

I'LL LET YOU LIVE A BIT LONGER IF YOU CUT OFF ANOTHER.

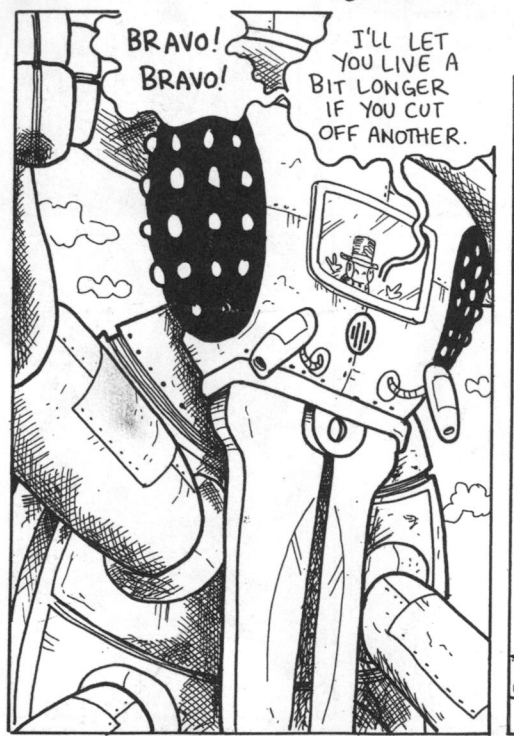

no time for... unh...for that...

this is the part of my **master plan** where...

unh.

...where dad takes you down and i...

unh.

...i save my family...

BY LOPPING OFF YOUR HAND?

had to break contact with your big, fat metal fingers because ..unh.. ..when i built dad's robot body.. ..i..unh.. i kept in mind that he ..unh.. loves puns.

WHAT IS **THAT** SUPPOSED TO MEAN?

..You're not **just** a firefly.. ..are you, dad..?

WHAT DO YOU—?

WHHIRRR CLICK

ACCESSING

HA!

WELL, WOULD YOU LOOK AT THAT...

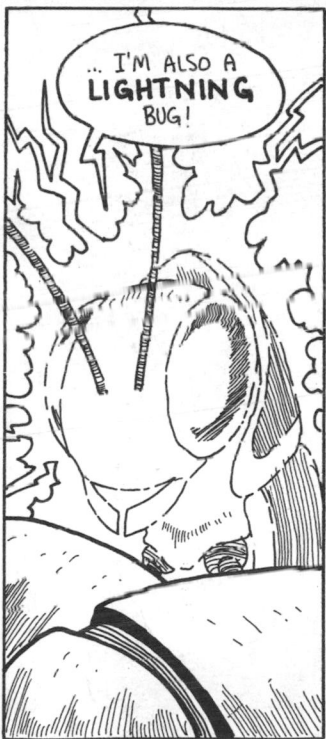

..I'M ALSO A **LIGHTNING** BUG!

IN FACT, Y'KNOW WHAT?

YOU'VE GOT IT **WORSE** THAN THE AMBER BEETLE.

YOU WANT ALL OF US TO BE STUCK **WITH** YOU.

BAH! SPARE ME THE CALLOW "INSIGHTS" OF YOUTH.

I AM PROTECTING OUR WORLD.

PFFT! YOU'RE PROTECTING **YOUR** WORLD. **OUR** WORLD IS SO MUCH BIGGER AND FULL OF WONDERS, INCLUDING THE MOST AMAZING BEETLES I'VE EVER SEEN.

THEY'RE SKITTERING SAVAGES.

THEY'RE **OUR FAMILY.**

YOU MAY TRACE YOUR HERITAGE TO THOSE BEASTS, BUT DO NOT PRESUME TO BRING US ALL SO LOW.

I WAS SHAPED BY SCARABUS TO BE SOMETHING GREATER.

RIIIIIGHT. IGNORE REALITY AND GO WITH THE MAGICAL STORY THAT MAKES YOU SPECIAL.

I AM YOUR BETTER IN EVERY WAY, GIRL.

SAYS THE BEETLE TRAPPED IN HIS GIANT ROBOT.

READY TO GO, DAD?

YOU BETCHA!

STOP!

ONE MORE STEP AND YOU'RE DEAD.

earlier..
..when you were talking to my sister..

..you misspoke..

..what you meant to say to her was:

"You haven't won YET."

groaann..

WE SHOULD HURRY, MOSSY. I WOULD PREFER NOT TO BE HERE **DURING** THE EXPLOSION.

CAN I **LEAVE** HIM?

ONLY IF YOU WANT TO **BECOME** HIM, DEAR.

sigh

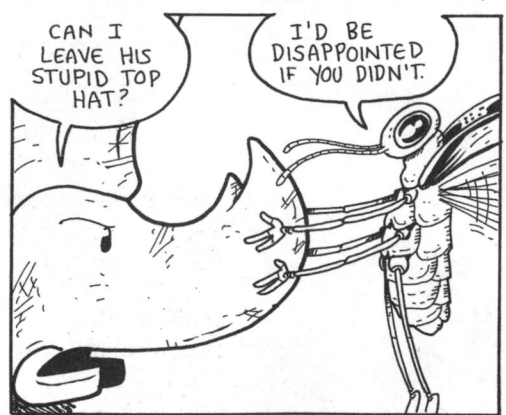

CAN I LEAVE HIS STUPID TOP HAT?

I'D BE DISAPPOINTED IF YOU DIDN'T.

EXCELLENT. THAT'LL DRIVE OWEN NUTS.

TSK.

YOU ARE **SO** BAD.

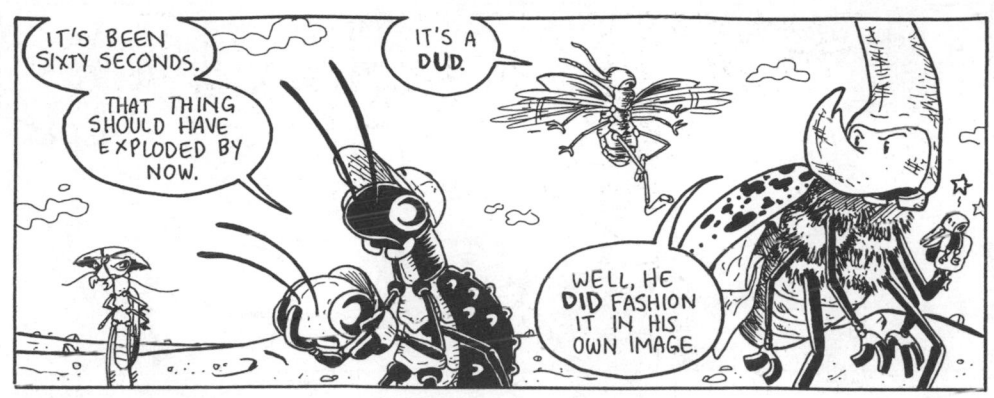

IT'S BEEN SIXTY SECONDS.

THAT THING SHOULD HAVE EXPLODED BY NOW.

IT'S A **DUD**.

WELL, HE **DID** FASHION IT IN HIS OWN IMAGE.

OH, DEAR. LET ME SEE.

IT'S ALREADY HEALING, MOM.

THESE ARE THE BENEFITS OF A COMPARTMENTALIZED EXOSKELETON AND A LOW-PRESSURE CIRCULATORY SYSTEM.

PLUS, Y'KNOW, GOOD CLOTTING FACTORS.

IT'S A PRETTY COOL SYSTEM.

IT'S AMAZING.

CAN WE GO NOW?

I AIN'T GOIN' ANOTHER DING-BLASTED STEP UNTIL SOMEONE EXPLAINS HOW...**THAT**... IS POSSIBLE.

AH, THE STORY OF HOW I GOT MY ROBOT BODY. IT'S A DOOZY!

WE'LL TELL YOU ON THE WALK HOME.

SPEAKING OF WHICH...

Chapter 15

WHEN WE LEFT ON THIS EXPEDITION, WE WANDERED THE DESERT FOR THREE DAYS BEFORE DISCOVERING THE GIANT BONES.

USING RAEF'S NAVIGATION SYSTEM, THE TRIP BACK TO THE OASIS FROM THE SAME SPOT WAS A STRAIGHT SHOT. WE WERE HOME IN LESS THAN A DAY.

LONG BEFORE WE REACHED THE CITY GATE, I SAW MY BONES RISING OVER THE OASIS.

THE ARCHITECT OF THIS MONSTROSITY NEVER REGAINED CONSCIOUSNESS DURING OUR TRIP HOME.

OWEN WOKE UP IN A CELL, BUT HE DIDN'T STAY THERE LONG. HE HAS TOO MANY FRIENDS IN HIGH PLACES AND HE JUST SLIPPED AWAY.

MORIARTY DETENTION CENTER

AS FAR AS MY FAMILY IS CONCERNED, OUR RETURN HAS MEANT SIGNIFICANT CHANGES IN OUR LIVES. WE HAVE COLLEAGUES CRAWLING OUT OF THE WOODWORK TO HEAR ABOUT THE NATURAL WONDERS WE'VE SEEN.

ONE EVEN CRAWLED OUT OF THE GROUND.

MIRIAM?

cough hello?

MOM HAS BEEN PUT IN CHARGE OF OWEN'S SECRET LAB IN THE OLD CITY. THE QUEEN HAS COMMISSIONED HER TO TURN IT INTO A RESEARCH FACILITY FOR THOSE INTERESTED IN EXPLORATION.

WE EACH HAVE OUR OWN LAB NOW AND THE FIRST THING I DID WAS BUILD DAD A NEW BODY.

CAN WE PUT IN AN ICE CREAM DISPENSOR?

OKAY, BUT WE'LL NEED TO REMOVE THE GUMBALL MACHINE.

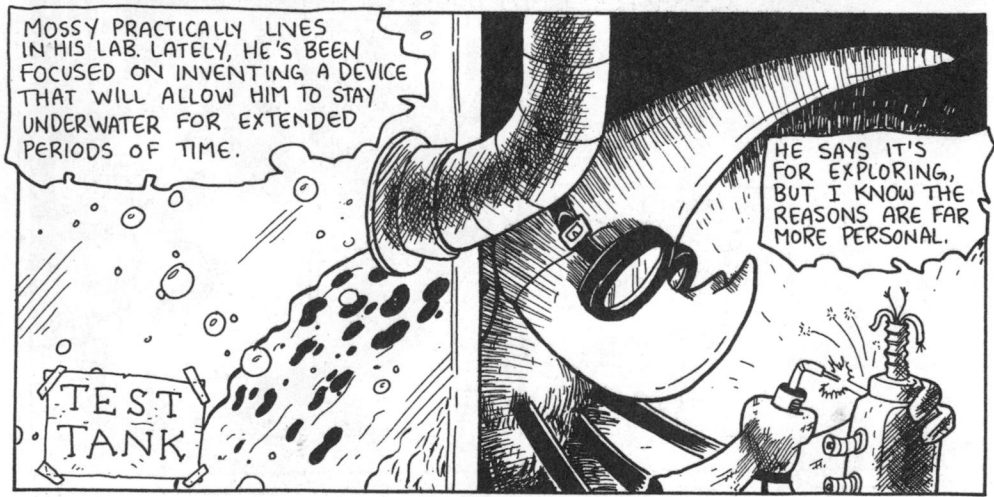

MOSSY PRACTICALLY LIVES IN HIS LAB. LATELY, HE'S BEEN FOCUSED ON INVENTING A DEVICE THAT WILL ALLOW HIM TO STAY UNDERWATER FOR EXTENDED PERIODS OF TIME.

HE SAYS IT'S FOR EXPLORING, BUT I KNOW THE REASONS ARE FAR MORE PERSONAL.

TEST TANK

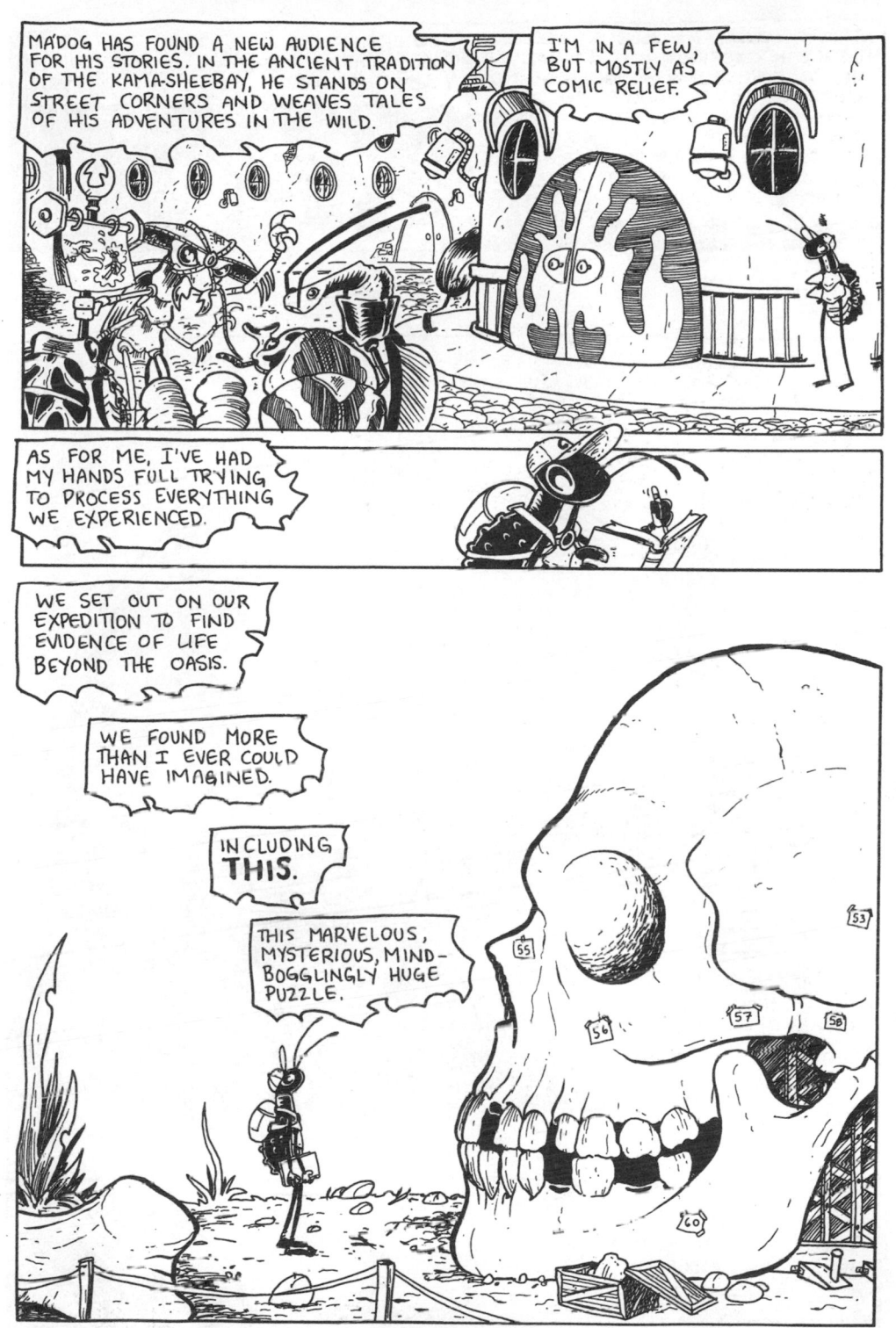

WE'VE TAKEN APART OWEN'S "CAGE-BEAST" AND ARE IN THE PROCESS OF PUTTING IT TOGETHER CORRECTLY. IT IS AMAZINGLY IMMENSE. AND WHILE THE EPIC SCALE OF THIS CREATURE BLOWS MY MIND, THE MONUMENTAL SIZE ISN'T THE COOLEST THING ABOUT MY BONES.

AT THE BOTTOM OF THE HEAD BONES THERE IS A HOLE AND INSIDE THAT HOLE IS A CHAMBER.

A HUGE CHAMBER.

I THINK IT MIGHT HAVE BEEN FOR THE BRAIN. YOU CAN ALMOST FEEL THE ECHOES OF IDEAS SWIRLING AROUND AND BUZZING OFF THE WALLS.

I FIND MYSELF THINKING ABOUT THIS HUE-MON ALL OF THE TIME. I WONDER IF IT EVER THOUGHT ABOUT US?

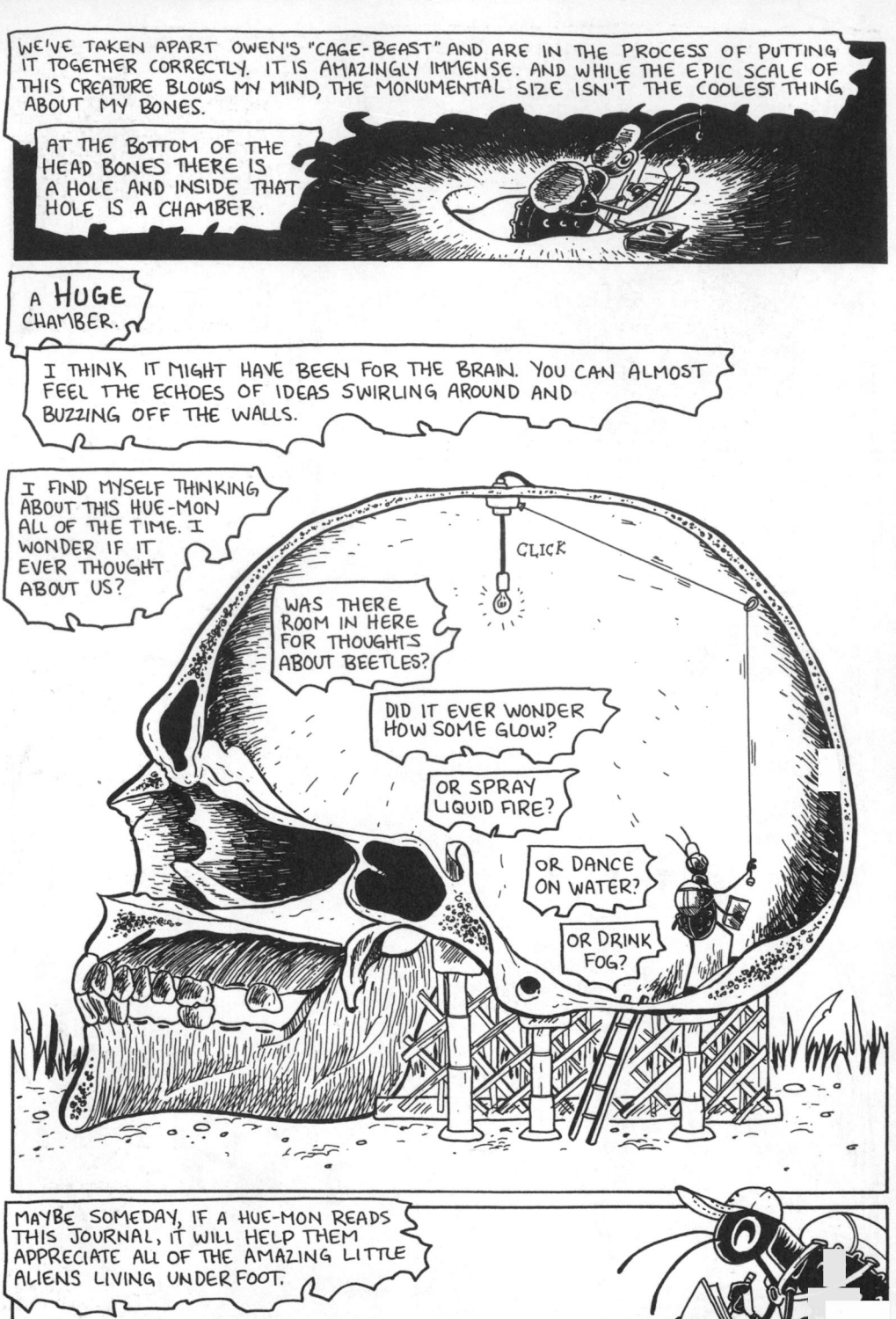

CLICK

WAS THERE ROOM IN HERE FOR THOUGHTS ABOUT BEETLES?

DID IT EVER WONDER HOW SOME GLOW?

OR SPRAY LIQUID FIRE?

OR DANCE ON WATER?

OR DRINK FOG?

MAYBE SOMEDAY, IF A HUE-MON READS THIS JOURNAL, IT WILL HELP THEM APPRECIATE ALL OF THE AMAZING LITTLE ALIENS LIVING UNDER FOOT.

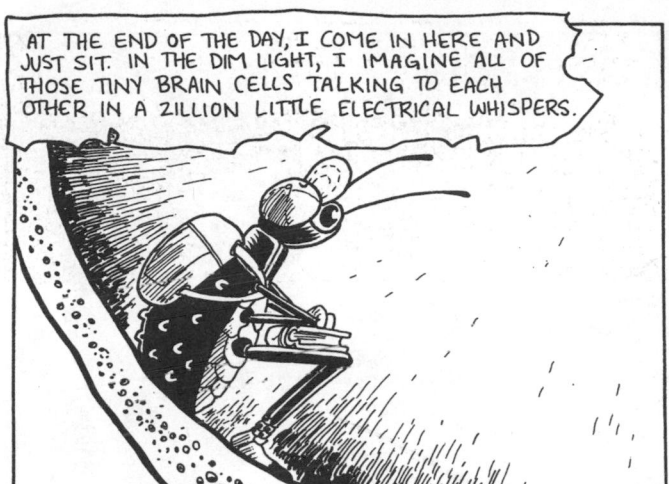

AT THE END OF THE DAY, I COME IN HERE AND JUST SIT. IN THE DIM LIGHT, I IMAGINE ALL OF THOSE TINY BRAIN CELLS TALKING TO EACH OTHER IN A ZILLION LITTLE ELECTRICAL WHISPERS.

I NEVER HAVE TO STAY LONG.

A FEW MINUTES OF WONDER IS ENOUGH TO RECHARGE MY IMAGINATION AND PREPARE ME FOR THE NEXT AMAZING, UNEXPECTED THING.

BOOGA BOOGA!

GAH!

DAG-GONE IT, DAD! WHAT DID I TELL YOU ABOUT SCARING ME?

OH, DON'T BE SUCH A FUSSBUDGET.

BESIDES, WHAT ARE YOU GONNA DO ABOUT IT?

something I swore I would never do again...

Annotations

Chapter 1

Page 1: Our journey starts on an auspicious date. Just ask my sister.

Page 3: Scarabus gets his name from the scarab beetles. Scarabs were sacred to the ancient Egyptians who believed a dung beetle rolled the sun across the heavens. Scarabs can be gorgeously iridescent colors, so it probably isn't surprising that they feature prominently in Egyptian art. If you want to see plates and plates of scarabs along with other beetle beauties, check out the book *Living Jewels* by Poul Beckmann.

Page 5: Antennae are the perfect symbol of exploration. They contain the sensory apparatus an insect needs to taste, smell, and touch the environment. They can also be used to sense humidity and gauge air speed when the insect is flying. They are an insect's tongue, nose, finger, divining rod, and speedometer all in one.

Chapter 2

Page 11: Chill-coma was the focus of my graduate work. It is a reversible condition that occurs when an insect's muscles (and probably nerves) lose their resting electrical potential at low temperatures. As a result, they are no longer able to effectively send signals and contract muscles. Eventually the insect becomes immobile and tips over. The process is reversible, however. Warm 'em up and they spring back to life (assuming you haven't left them cold for too long—then they're just dead). You can read all about it in the thrilling paper by Hosler, Burns, and Esch, "Flight Muscle Resting Potential and Species-Specific Differences in Chill-coma," *Journal of Insect Physiology* 46, no. 5 (2000) : 621–7.

Page 13: By treating their sleeping bags with nasty chemicals to dissuade predators, it looks like Professor Bombardier knows a thing or two about chemical ecology. If I didn't know better, I would swear she had read *Secret Weapons* by one of the founders of the field of chemical ecology, Thomas Eisner.

Pages 16–17: Lucy is modeled after the tenebrionid beetle *Stenocara sp.* that lives in the Namib Desert. The water-catching apparatus on *Stenocara*'s elytra works as described in the story and is detailed in the article called "Water Capture by a Desert Beetle" in the journal *Nature*. These fog-catching beetles have fused elytra. *Stenocara* is only about 1 cm wide, so Lucy is probably a bit bigger than the beetle that inspired her.

Page 17: When I was interviewing for faculty positions, I had the opportunity to meet several interesting faculty and provosts at various institutions. (I met so many because no one wanted to hire me.) At one institution, I had a memorable conversation with a provost who repeatedly told me that I must not *condense* to the students. I'm pretty sure he met *condescend* since it would never occur to me to spit or otherwise splash water on students. That was one of the few job offers I got, and I turned them down.

Page 18: Professor Owen is named after Richard Owen, the great Victorian anatomist and adversary of Charles Darwin. He is modeled loosely on the flightless Cape Stag Beetle (*Colophon primosi*), but would be smaller than the real deal. The natural history of *Colophon primosi* has not been well studied and that isn't going to get any easier. Its population numbers have been so heavily impacted by beetle collectors that *Colophon primosi* is banned from international sales, and export.

Page 19: Tracheae are breathing tubes that branch throughout the body of an insect. Air enters these tubes through small holes called *spicules* that are found along the sides of the insect (imagine these as nostrils on its abdomen). Insects typically can't inhale and exhale like you and me, so oxygen moves passively through these tubes. Because of this, it would probably be difficult for a beetle to play a wind instrument because that requires highly controlled exhalations of air. However, in the article "Tracheal Respiration in Insects Visualized with Synchrotron X-ray Imaging" (2003), Mark Westneat and his colleagues report on a beetle that makes periodic contractions of its trachea, allowing it to move air through its trachea actively. So, maybe Lucy could do it after all, but clearly not very well. Nevertheless, I needed to include some music in this story for my mom. If she had been in the desert with our heroes, she could have announced the day with an epic trombone solo!

Page 21: The horned viper *Cerastes cerastes* lies in wait under the sand for passing prey. Its scientific name comes from Cerastes, the serpent from Greek mythology that hunted its victims in the same fashion.

Page 21, Panel 8: Lucy's elytra are fused, so she can't open them to pop her wings out. This is why she cannot fly.

Page 27: In my office I have a colony of flour beetles that have been living on my desk for the last four years. They do not fly away and get all of their nourishment and water from the flour they live in. They live their whole life cycle there and routinely burrow into the flour to get away from me.

Chapter 3
Page 33: These pages were done while I was an assistant professor at Juniata College. Clearly, ongoing concerns about tenure and job security offered some inspiration for this scene.

Page 39: Insects use pheromones for a wide array of things. Bees use them to alert the hive of danger, ants use them to mark trails, and moths use them to find mates. Specifically, females will signal their willingness to mate by releasing a pheromone cue into the air. Males can pick up this signal from miles away and home in on it with pinpoint accuracy. This is even more impressive when you bear in mind that this usually happens at night, when it is impossible for the moth to see anything. You know that the moths in this scene are males because of their highly branched antennae. This branching makes it more likely for them to pick up the female's faint pheromone signal. In contrast, female moths usually have thin, unbranched antennae. Female moths don't need to go looking for love; it comes to them.

Page 41: The town we live in was founded where the Standing Stone Creek runs into the Juniata River. There is a Standing Stone Monument downtown that commemorates a similar monolith that was used by local Indian tribes. It doesn't seem to be clear from historical accounts if the monument was a crossroads marker or if it traveled with migrating tribes. In any event, it is a symbol of our community and marks the place we call home.

Chapter 4

Pages 53–54: The robotic interface we have on these moths may look futuristic, but it really isn't. Researchers have already developed a cyborg beetle that wears a computer chip on its back and has wires implanted into its brain. Scientists can actually activate specific brain regions and control specific behaviors such as flight and turning. Don't believe me? Check out the article "Cyborg Beetles" from the December 2010 issue of *Scientific American*. It has pictures.

Page 56: Ocean and lake water are often filled with dissolved nutrients, microorganisms, plankton, and bits of dead things floating around. Under these conditions, it isn't surprising to find suspension-feeding organisms that live at the bottom of a body of water feeding on whatever might drift down their way. It's a bit more surprising to find suspension feeders on land. Air has far fewer nutrients and organic junk floating around in it. Nevertheless, this is where orb spiders make their living, surviving on anything that might be unlucky enough to drift into their sticky webs.

Page 57: Spiders liquefy their prey because they have no chewing mouthparts. They can sting and paralyze prey, but they can't break it into small chunks and grind it up. Instead, they inject their prey with enzymes that digest their victims before they consume them.

Page 57, Panel 9: Spiders and insects often have abundant taste receptors on their feet. In some cases the ability to taste with your feet can be different between males and females of the same species. In the paper "Female Behaviour Drives Expression and Evolution of Gustatory Receptors in Butterflies," Adriana Briscoe and her colleagues show that female butterflies of the species *Heliconius melpomene* have extensive taste receptors on their feet but males don't. The females need to be able to sense toxic chemicals in plants so that they can identify safe plants on which they can lay their eggs. It is published in *PLoS Genetics* and features a two-page comic about the butterflies that the author commissioned from me.

Page 58: Spiders will cut things from their webs if they are not edible. In his book *For Love of Insects*, Thomas Eisner discusses how the spider *Nephila clavipes* will cut the moth *Utethesia ornatrix* from its web because the moth tastes nasty. When the moth hits the web, it doesn't struggle. As if anticipating the inevitable, it remains motionless and waits for the spider to set it free.

Page 58, Panel 8: Many spiders spin a new web every night and consume the web in the morning to recycle the silk. To examine how much, if any, of the silk from the old web is recycled, Mark A. Townley and Edward K. Tillinghast fed spiders radioactive 14C-glucose. The 14C was incorporated into the spiders' silk and eventually into their webs. Amazingly, when the spiders consume old webs they can solubilize almost all of the silk proteins and reuse up to 32% of them as soon as thirty minutes later. In an earlier paper, D. B. Peakall placed a spider (*Araneus*) on a radioactive web that was labeled with [3H] alanine. When the spider consumed the web, Peakall saw a much higher recycling rate, reporting that the spiders recycled 80–90% of the silk proteins within thirty minutes of ingestion.

Page 65, Panel 4: My appreciation of an insect's ability to fall from great heights without getting hurt started when I saw a news story on the invasive plant, purple loosestrife. Purple loosestrife is native to Europe, where it's kept in check by its natural enemy, the black-margined loosestrife beetle. To combat the spread of purple loosestrife in North America, farmers in the US and Canada flew over their fields and dumped boxes of black-margined loosestrife beetles from the helicopter. You can't do that with mammals...

Page 65: I have very fond memories of watching Chicago Cubs games with my parents during my summer breaks in college. Although Lucy's hat looks just like my Cubs hat, hers is actually a Coleopolis Grubs cap.

Chapter 5

Page 78: Dyna-Soar is a (rather obvious) nod to the proud evolutionary lineage of birds. A sparrow probably looks like a T. Rex when you're the size of a beetle. Actually, it would look like a *flying* T. Rex, which is waaaaay worse.

Page 79: Amber is hardened tree resin, and organisms trapped in it provide an exciting glimpse into ancient life. The vast majority of these critters are insects, although there are examples of geckos, feathers, and frogs.

Insects in amber were all the rage in the 1990s when the book and movie *Jurassic Park* hit the scene. In the story, scientists extract dinosaur DNA from the guts of mosquitos trapped in amber. This DNA is used to reconstruct dinosaur genomes and bring them to life in a dinosaur theme park. Hilarity ensues. Much as I would love to see a live dinosaur, it doesn't look like we will be getting one from insects in amber. A recent study by David Penny, et al., used next-generation DNA sequencing techniques to show that even under the best conditions, researchers couldn't extract enough DNA to build a single gene, much less all of the genetic instructions needed to build a Brachiosaurus. The paper, published in *PLoS ONE*, is open-access and free for download.

Page 84: Willard Frank Libby won the 1960 Nobel Prize for developing radiocarbon dating. This technique allows scientists to use predictable rates of radioactive decay to determine how old a fossil is. MIT has a nice biography of Libby at www.nobelprize.org/nobel_prizes/chemistry/laureates/1960/libby-bio.html

Chapter 6

Page 98, Panel 1: That was a plant in my office I used for reference. It didn't last long after this drawing. Apparently they need to be watered. Regularly.

Page 98, Panel 2: This is my homage to Osamu Tezuka's *Astro Boy*. His cross-section drawings of Astro Boy were always inspiring. Tezuka was a remarkable cartoonist, producing thousands of pages of comics in his life and a stunning library of graphic fiction. He is particularly near and dear to my heart because he was originally trained as a doctor and had a great love of insects. When he was fifteen, he published *A Color Picture Book of Beetles*. Check out *The Art of Osamu Tezuka, God of Manga* by Helen McCarthy to see stunning examples of beetle drawings.

Page 102: Approximately 40% of all insect species are beetles, and about 30% of all animal species on the planet are beetles. By comparison, all of the fish, amphibians, reptiles, birds, and mammals, on Earth comprise only 3–5% of all known animal species. Why are the beetles so successful? It may be their elytra. Most insects have two pairs of wings. In beetles, the front pair of wings have evolved into elytra, a hard covering that protects the back wings. Giving up a pair of functional wings would suggest that elytra offered a unique evolutionary advantage that was more useful than the wings themselves. Perhaps the elytra's protection allows beetles to skitter into rough hidey-holes that insects with unprotected, delicate wings might not? Or maybe they were a good defense against predators? Either way, it was undoubtedly a big factor in their success.

Page 108: Raef gets his name from my two grandfathers, Raphael and Ralf, and is based on the firefly *Photinus pyralis*. He gets his blinky bottom through the action of the enzyme luciferase. Luciferase derives its name from that of the fallen angel Lucifer, whose name means "shining one, morning star." There are several different species that contain luciferase, including fireflies, click beetles, mushrooms, small aquatic arthropods, and sea pansies. The Wikipedia page for luciferase is a great place to start to get a sense of how the reaction works and what organisms use it.

Chapter 7

Page 116: *Nicrophorus* are carrion-burying beetles. These beetles make sound in a way similar to crickets. Crickets rub the edges of their wings together in a process called *stridulation*. One wing has a bumpy file and another has a hard scraper. When the cricket draws the scaper across the file quickly, it makes the *zzit* sound we love listening to on a warm summer night. *Nicrophorus* have their files and scrapers on their elytra and stridulate during copulation, to deter predators, and to communicate with their larvae. I discovered the story of *Nicrophorus* for the first time in the excellent book *An Inordinate Fondness for Beetles* by Arthur Evans and Charles Bellamy.

Page 118: Most beetles provide very limited parental care, but the *Nicrophorus* do a lot for their kids. Either the male or female will bury a carcass and then wait for a mate to arrive. In some cases, individual beetles will move a much larger carcass several meters to find a better burial spot. Once together, the male and female work together to build a nest, predigest the food for their grubs, and stay with the young until they pupate.

Page 121: Many insects can consume and store toxic chemicals in their bodies. This is a terrific way of protecting yourself from predators. Couple that with some bright color-ation, and you can send a clear signal to a potential predator that you taste awful. Ask any blue jay. Monarch butterflies taste awful!

Page 122: The headspring is another nod to Tezuka's *Astro Boy*.

Page 121: Many animals have codes that they use to communicate with members of their own species. Sometimes these signals are odors (ants), song (crickets), or touch (fruit fly mating). In the case of fireflies, males and females find each other using species-specific pulses of light. This makes it possible for itty-bitty fireflies to find an itty-bitty mate in a gigantic field at night. Since the signal is so specific, it also helps them save time by not chasing light signals from the wrong species. This is usually a reliable system. However, any signal that is this specific is prone to exploitation. The firefly species *Photuris* will mimic the light signal of the firefly *Photinus* and lure the male *Photinus* to its death. It is a sad story of the male *Photinus* looking for love in all the wrong places.

Page 126: Well, now we know how the professor survived the snake. Professor Bombar-dier is a bombardier beetle. Her appearance is based on a photograph from Thomas Eisner's *Secret Weapons* (page 157). The caption under the image indicates the pictured bombardier beetle is an unidentified South American species. Bombardier beetles gener-ate their noxious squirt in a two-step process. They have a reservoir containing reactive chemicals. When disturbed, the beetle releases these chemicals into a reaction chamber that contains a mixture of enzymes. These enzymes set off a series of chemical reactions that results in a blazing spray.

My favorite bombardier beetle story is from Charles Darwin's *Autobiography*. Beetle collecting was all the rage in Victorian England, and Darwin was very good at it. Here is how he relates the incident in his autobiography:

One day, on tearing off some old bark, I saw two rare beetles and seized one in each hand; then I saw a third and new kind, which I could not bear to lose, so that I popped the one which I held in my right hand into my mouth. Alas it ejected some intensely acrid fluid, which burnt my tongue so that I was forced to spit the beetle out, which was lost, as well as the third one. —Charles Darwin

In recent years, creationists have argued that the complexity of the bombardier beetles' firing mechanism must have been designed. These arguments are systematically refuted by Mark Isaak in *The Counter-Creationism Handbook*.

Dr. Bombardier gets her first name Beatrice from the character Beatrice who was one of Dante's guides through Hell. While our heroes aren't exactly in Hades, Dr. Bombardier does provide a steadying influence under stressful conditions.

Page 129: Lucy was just on the verge of discovering the concept of homology. A homologous trait is a characteristic that two species share because they have a common ancestor that had that trait. So, why do amphibians, reptiles, birds, and mammals all have four limbs? Because we all descended from an ancient fishy thing that crawled onto land on four limbs.

Chapter 8

Page 148: Bats emit ultrasonic calls to navigate and hunt. They listen for the echoes of their calls to determine how far away an object is and in what direction it is moving. Since bats hunt insects, it isn't surprising that many insects have evolved the ability to detect and evade bats' ultrasonic calls. In addition to some beetles, numerous butterflies, moths, and lacewings can do this neat trick.

Page 150: If you want to see a velvet worm's snot guns in action, check out the "Invasion of Land" episode of David Attenborough's excellent series *Life in the Undergrowth*.

Chapter 9

Page 161: Miriam is modeled after the burrowing beetle (*Mycotrupes gaigei*). This is a relatively small beetle found living in sandy soil. An extensive survey of populations in Florida was published in 1954 by Ada L. Olson, T. H. Hubbel, and H. F. Howden. Miriam's last name is "Bedlow" because she makes her home (and bed, presumably) in an underground burrow. In their study, Olson, Hubbel, and Howden found active burrows that extended almost seven feet below ground. Looks like digging is in Miriam's blood (or hemolymph, as the case may be…).

Page 164: As Keith Thomson points out in *Before Darwin*, as we became more and more aware of fossils early in our history, humans that believed the earth was created in seven days tried to make sense of fossils by describing them as "formed stones" that only resembled living things.

Page 168: Purporting to use science to try to find evidence of the divine is an all too common occurrence. The most prominent recent example of this was the unsuccessful Intelligent Design movement.

Chapter 10

Page 184, Panel 2: Nobody has ever drawn machines like Jack Kirby. While the inner workings of Tezuka's *Astro Boy* inspired me, Jack Kirby's machines blew my mind. They were like looking at schematics from another dimension far in our future. Raef's head was designed by Tezuka, but his heart is all Kirby.

Page 185: My eldest son Max said this to me when he was three or four. He has an uncanny way of seeing the world as a scientist and a poet all at the same time. This phrase also shoots through my head when I'm hugging someone I love.

Page 188: Have you ever tried to catch a whirligig? They're like drops of oil skittering across the surface of a skillet. They swim in large clusters at the water's edge, and there is something irresistibly joyous in the motions.

Page 189: Whirligigs may be tiny and cute, but they are far from defenseless. They can secrete a noxious chemical called *gyrinidal* that will make a fish spit them right out. You can read all about it in *Secret Weapons*.

Page 190: In the 1970s, my family faithfully watched *Happy Days* and *Laverne and Shirley*. It was in the latter that I first heard the song "High Hopes," whose lyrics tell of an ant that wants to move a rubber tree plant. Of course, everyone knows an ant can't move a rubber tree plant, but he has high hopes.

Page 190: Ma'dog is telling a tale of marauder ants. The little sisters are called "minors" and the big sisters are "majors." There are a number of excellent books on ants out there, but for marauder ants check out *Adventures Among Ants* by the myrmecologist and photographer Mark Moffett.

Page 191: There are several good books about social insects available. Let me recommend a few. For ants, *The Leafcutter Ants: Civilization by Instinct* by Bert Hölldobler and E. O. Wilson is an interesting and accessible introduction to one of the most complex ant societies. If you want to ease into ants with a beautiful comic/picture book, I highly recommend *Cyberantics: A Little Adventure* by Jerry Prosser, Rick Geary, and Stanislaw Mayakovsky. To learn more about bees, my-go to book is *The Biology of the Honey Bee* by Mark Winston. I read this as a graduate student and couldn't put it down. It was ultimately the inspiration for *Clan Apis*, my graphic novel biography about a honey bee named Nyuki. It will come as no surprise to anyone that I think *Clan Apis* is a worthwhile place to start if you prefer to learn about bees through comics.

Page 192: These lyrics are taken from the song "Follow Me" by the band Bearfoot Bluegrass. We had the opportunity to see Bearfoot Bluegrass perform as part of Juniata College's Artist series. It was a special treat because my mom and dad were in town, so we could take them as well. Last time I checked, they still had the album *Follow Me* in their car.

Page 193: There is a lot of my younger son in Mossy. When someone gets hurt, Jack is right there to help. When his friend got hit in the face with a soccer ball during a match, Jack ran to him and cradled him in his arms until we flat-footed adults woke up and came to help. Just last year, he ran into the midst of a torrent of sledding kids to protect a first grader who had gotten upended by a reckless kid on an inner tube. Mossy was the nickname of Lisa's grandfather DeMoss. Interestingly enough, after he had passed away, the family discovered his real name was Adam. Go figure. He is modeled after *Dynastes hercules*.

Chapter 11

Page 207, Panel 2: The diving bell spider, *Argyroneta aquatica*, uses silk strands to build an underwater bubble house. Using tiny hairs on its abdomen and legs, the diving bell spider pulls bubbles of air from the water surface down into the web. Females spend most of their time in the bubble, but males spend a lot of their time swimming and hunting in the water.

Page 209: Eliza is based on the diving beetle *Dytiscus*. I first heard about diving beetles in the Comparative Physiology class I took in graduate school. This was one of my favorite classes of all time, chock-full of cool things, but the way diving beetles breathe is easily the coolest thing I remember about it. Estimates suggest that if the diving beetle was swimming near the surface, oxygen diffusing into the bubble would provide up to seven times as much oxygen found in the initial bubble. If the beetle dives too deeply, water pressure will drive oxygen out of the bubble, causing the bubble to collapse.

Chapter 12

Page 221: I once heard an ant biologist describe ants as the nastiest creatures in the world. Piles of ant bodies can be found where the territory of one colony meets the territory of another. And, as if fighting wasn't bad enough, some species specialize in enslaving other species by capturing larvae from neighboring nests and raising the young as their minions.

Page 222: The little rove beetle is named Bugs after my favorite trickster, Bugs Bunny. My dad and I used to watch Bugs Bunny cartoons any chance we could get. Most incarnations of Bugs are of that rascally rabbit that only messes with others when provoked. However, in his early appearances, Bugs was a bit of a jerk, often seeking confrontation for no reason. My Bugs is much closer to the early Bugs Bunny. He's also got a touch of Brer Rabbit to him, now that I think of it.

Page 222, Panel 6: As I mentioned earlier, predators and parasites can crack the codes animals use to communicate with each other. The rove beetle and a host of other insects (wasps, butterflies, and other beetles, for starters) have evolved ways to exploit the pheromone communication cues of ants. Pheromones are chemicals released by one organism that alter the behavior of another organism. For example, larvae of the Alcon Blue butterfly are cared for by ants because the butterfly larvae emit an odor that mimics ant larvae smells. This is detailed beautifully in the "Intimate Relations" episode of *Life in the Undergrowth*. As Bugs notes, living safe and sound underground with a nearly unlimited food supply is a pretty sweet set up for a relatively defenseless insect larva.

Page 226: Ant nests can be unbelievably big. A group of researchers led by Luis Forgi poured concrete into an abandoned leaf-cutter ant colony and then excavated it a month later. What they found was a colony that was 50 square meters in size and extended 26 feet underground. See *The Leafcutter Ants* for cool pictures.

Page 227: Having millions of ants in a colony means there is plenty of fodder to throw at a potential attacker. Losing a head here or there is a small sacrifice in the overall scheme of things. In fact, for those that consider ant colonies to be superorganisms, losing a single ant would be like you sloughing a few skin cells to deflect the claw of a cat. The superorganism is an intriguing way to think about social insects like ants. In their book *Journey to the Ants*, Wilson and Hölldobler once famously wrote that "One ant alone is a disappointment; it is really no ant at all." In other words, so much of what it means to be an ant is tied up in what the ants accomplish together. This scene was inspired by photos of beetles wearing ant heads on their limbs as mementoes of an earlier confrontation (*For Love of Insects*, page 260).

Page 229: Bugs is based on the myrmecophilus ("ant-loving") beetle *Atemeles pubicollis*. Check out the chapter "Social Parasites" in *Journey to the Ants* for the full lowdown on this beetle. Pay special attention to the figures on pages 139 and 140. They were the visual references I used to create this behavior interaction.

Page 230: Telescoping arms are the greatest piece of impossible sci-fi technology ever. My favorites were the creeping tentacles of Dr. Octopus as drawn by the incomparable Steve Ditko.

Page 234: Cokie is modeled after a ladybug beetle in the genus *Coccinella*. I shortened that name and adopted the spelling "Cokie" in honor of Cokie Roberts, one of our favorite news commentators.

Page 236: In the mid-1970s, I had to wear a husky pair of Garanimals pants. It was a memorable experience.

Chapter 13

Page 246: This page was done during Lisa's first night in the hospital when she had a perforated appendix. Professor Bombardier's dialogue reflects a tiny sliver of Lisa's distress.

Page 247: I've always had trouble drawing butterflies. This is in large part because I never really looked at one very closely. So, this page was done using a specimen from the insect collection that is housed in my Invertebrate Biology teaching lab. They really are quite pretty.

Page 252: There is a stunning array of insect species sailing above you right now. For a nice explanation of this phenomenon, see the chapter entitled "Air" in Hugh Raffles's book *Insectopedia*. If you prefer storytelling and animation, check out Robert Krulwich's piece for NPR called "Look Up! The Billion-Bug Highway You Can't See." The link is in the references.

Page 253: The bigger you are, the slower you cool and the slower you warm up. That's because the bigger you are, the more volume you have (everything just under the surface of your skin) relative to your surface area (your skin). It is easier for small things to lose the heat in their bodies because all of their guts are relatively close to their surface. However, as things get bigger, their volume increases by a power of three (cubic measurement) but their surface area only increases by a power of two (square measurement). Mathematically speaking, an organism's volume increases faster than its surface area. This means that most of the guts of a very big animal are relatively far away from the animal's surface, making it easier for it to hold on to heat.

Page 255: It was tempting to drop dozens of Beatles puns in a book about beetles. This is the only one I allowed myself.

Chapter 14

Page 263: Giant robots are cool, even when they're evil. My personal favorites are Mechagodzilla and Gigantor.

Page 273: Cryptobiosis is the remarkable ability of some organisms to survive extreme conditions in a state resembling suspended animation. The all-time best critter at cryptobiosis is not an insect, but a related critter called a *tardigrade* (or, more commonly, "water bear"). These little beasts live in the water film on many plants and can survive extraordinary heat, cold, and desiccation. They even weather the inky void of space just fine. Tardigrades can lower their metabolisms to 1/600th of the normal rate. Owen's chamber clearly tapped into that biological phenomenon to keep Lucy's egg alive.

Page 276: Watching Lucy cut off her hand is hard because we couldn't do that quite as easily. In fact, we would bleed to death without prompt medical care. But insects routinely lose appendages and go about their business just fine. When I collect insects with a class or with the boys, we routinely find specimens missing one or two legs and maybe an antenna.

Page 280: In an 1860 Oxford debate on evolution with the biologist T. H. Huxley, Archbishop Wilberforce reportedly asked Huxley if he was descended from a monkey on his grandfather's or grandmother's side of the family. Huxley is said to have replied that he would rather be descended from a monkey than connected to a man (i.e., Wilberforce) who would use his oratorical gifts to obscure the truth. (J. R. Lucas, "Wilberforce and Huxley: A Legendary Encounter," *The Historical Journal* 22, no. 2 (June 1979):313–30.)

Page 282: Rhinocerus beetles are a type of Hercules beetle and, as the name implies, they are pretty strong. How strong? Poke around the Internet a bit, and you find several sites declaring that they can lift 850 times their own weight. This fact appears to trace back to *The Guinness Book of World Records*, but I couldn't find any scientific evidence supporting this figure. Neither could Rodger Kram, apparently. As detailed in Carl Zimmer's *Discover Magazine* article "Beetle of Burden," Kram read the same fact and set out to test it. His results, published in the *Journal of Experimental Biology*, indicate that the beetle can lift a whopping 100 times its weight. Not quite 850 times, but still impressive. The cool finding from this paper was that these beetles can carry this extra weight very efficiently, expending far less energy than traditional metabolic models would predict.

289, Panel 1: The desert ant *Cataglyphis fortis* has this remarkable ability. It will
the nest in the blazing midday sun and search for insect prey stunned by the heat.
search requires wandering about higgledy-piggledy, but once prey is found, the ant
rns around and heads straight back to the nest. To do this it must integrate information
about its direction from the colony with its distance from the colony. To gauge direction,
the ants use celestial cues like the sun. To determine distance from the colony, the ant
actually integrates the steps it takes during the foraging trip. Scientists determined this
by examining ants that had their legs shortened by cutting off the ends or lengthened by
gluing a horsehair stilt to each leg. They reported their results in a paper called "The Ant
Odometer: Stepping on Stilts and Stumps." *Science*, 312, (June 2006):1965–7.

Page 291: Manga Kamishibai (grossly English-ified in this book as Kama-Sheebay) is
a fascinating Japanese tradition that involves telling illustrated stories in public. The
practitioners of this paper theatre are called *Kamishibaiya*. The details of Ma'dog's craft
come from Eric P. Nash's *Manga Kamishibai*.

Page 293, Panel 5: The name *Lucy* has special meaning in this story. Both of my grand-
mothers were named Lucille, and Lisa's great-grandmother was Lucia. Max would have
been named Lucy if he had been born a girl. Lucy is also the name of *Australopithecus
afarensis*, the watershed hominid fossil discovered by paleoanthropologist Donald Johanson. I still have my copy of Johanson's book from the 1970s. The researchers were inspired to name the fossil Lucy because the Beatles song "Lucy in the Sky with Diamonds"
was playing as they celebrated their discovery. While the desert giant in this story isn't
an *Australopithecus*, it seemed appropriate that Lucy should find such a seminal human
fossil. This page features the last major Lucy reference in the book. Charles Schulz had
an enormous impact on my life and my desire to make comics. Lucy van Pelt, Charlie
Brown's football-snatching foil, is described by her mother as the world's greatest fussbudget.

References

Books

Beckmann, Poul. *Living Jewels: The Natural Design of Beetles*. Prestel Publishing: New York, NY.

Darwin, Charles. *The Autobiography of Charles Darwin* (reissue). W. W. Norton and Co.: New York, NY.

Eckert, Roger, David Randall, and George Augstine. *Animal Physiology*, 1st ed. W. H. Freeman and Co.: New York, NY.

Eisner, Thomas. *For Love of Insects*. The Belknap Press of Harvard University Press: Cambridge, MA.

Eisner, Thomas, Maria Eisner, and Melody Eisner. *Secret Weapons*. The Belknap Press of Harvard University Press: Cambridge, MA.

Evans, Arthur, and Charles Bellamy. *An Inordinate Fondness for Beetles*. Henry Holt and Co.: New York, NY.

Moffett, Mark. *Adventures Among Ants*. University of California Press: Berkeley, CA.

McCarthy, Helen. *The Art of Osamu Tezuka: God of Manga*. Abrams Comicarts: New York, NY.

Thomson, Keith. *Before Darwin*. Yale University Press: New Haven, CT.

Winston, Mark. *The Biology of the Honey Bee*. Harvard University Press: Cambridge, MA.

Hölldobler, Bert, and Edward O. Wilson. *Journey to the Ants: A Story of Scientific Exploration*. The Belknap Press of Harvard University Press: Cambridge, MA.

Hölldobler, Bert, and Edward O. Wilson. *The Leafcutter Ants: Civilization by Instinct*. W. W. Norton and Co.: New York, NY.

Hosler, Jay. *Clan Apis*. Active Synapse Comics: Columbus, OH.

Isaak, Mark. *The Counter-Creationism Handbook*. University of California Press: Berkeley, CA.

Nash, Eric P. *Manga Kamishibai: The Art of Japanese Paper Theater*. Abrams Comicarts: New York, NY.

Prosser, Jerry, Rick Geary, and Stanislaw Mayakovsky. *Cyberantics*. Dark Horse Comics: Milwaukie, OR.

Raffles, Hugh. *Insectopedia*. Vintage: New York, NY.

Articles

Briscoe A. D., Macias-Muñoz A., Kozak K. M., Walters J. R., Yuan F., et al. (2013). "Female Behaviour Drives Expression and Evolution of Gustatory Receptors in Butterflies." *PLoS Genetics*, July 11, 2013.

Chadwick, D. and M. Moffett (1998). "Planet of the Beetles." *National Geographic*, March 1998, vol. 193, no. 3.

Hosler J. S., Burns J. E., Esch H. E. (2000). "Flight Muscle Resting Potential and Species-specific Differences in Chill-coma." *Journal of Insect Physiology.* 46(5): 621–627.

Kram, R. (1996). "Inexpensive Load Carrying by Rhinoceros Beetles." *Journal of Experimental Biology*, 199 (Pt 3): 609–12.

Lucas, J. R. (1979). "Wilberforce and Huxley: a Legendary Encounter." *The Historical Journal*, Vol. 22, Issue 02 , pp. 313–330.

Maharbiz, Michel M. and Hirotaka Sato (2010). "Cyborg Beetles: Merging of Machine and Insect to Create Flying Robots." *Scientific American*, December 2010.

Olson, Ada L., T. H. Hubbell, and H. F. Howden (1954). "The Burrowing Beetles of the Genus *Mycotrupes* (Coleoptera: Scarabaeidae: Geotrupinae)." Miscellaneous Publications, Museum of Zoology, University of Michigan, No. 84.

Peakall, D. B. (1971). "Conservation of Web Proteins in the Spider *Araneus Diadematus.*" *Journal of Experimental Zoology*, Vol. 176, p. 257.

Penney, David, Caroline Wadsworth, Graeme Fox, Sandra L. Kennedy, Richard F. Preziosi, Terence A. Brown (2013). "Absence of Ancient DNA in Sub-Fossil Insect Inclusions Preserved in 'Anthropocene' Colombian Copal." *PLoS ONE*, September 11, 2013.

Scott, Michelle Pellissier (1998). "The Ecology and Behavior of Burying Beetles." *Annual Review of Entomology*, 43: 595–618.

Townley, Mark A. and Edward K. Tillinghast (1988). "Orb Web Recycling in *Araneus Cavaticus* (Araneae, Araneidae) with an Emphasis on the Adhesive Spiral Component, Gabamide." *Journal of Arachnology*, Vol. 16, No. 3, pp. 303–19.

Westneat, Mark W., Oliver Betz, Richard W. Blob, Kamel Fezzaa, W. James Cooper, and Wah-Keat Lee (2003). "Tracheal Respiration in Insects Visualized with Synchrotron X-ray Imaging." *Science*, January 24, 2003, Vol. 299, No. 5606, pp. 558–560.

Wittlinger, Matthias, Rüdiger Wehner, Harald Wolf (2006). "The Ant Odometer: Stepping on Stilts and Stumps." *Science*, Vol. 312, No. 5782, pp. 1965–1967.

Zimmer, Carl (1996). "Beetle of Burden." *Discover Magazine*, April issue.

Video

Life in the Undergrowth (2006). Hosted by David Attenborough. BBC Home Entertainment.

Look Up! The Billion-Bug Highway You Can't See. npr.org/blogs/ krulwich/2011/06/01/128389587/look-up-the-billion-bug-highway-you-cant-see.